WITCH TO THE END

A BLAIR WILKES MYSTERY

ELLE ADAMS

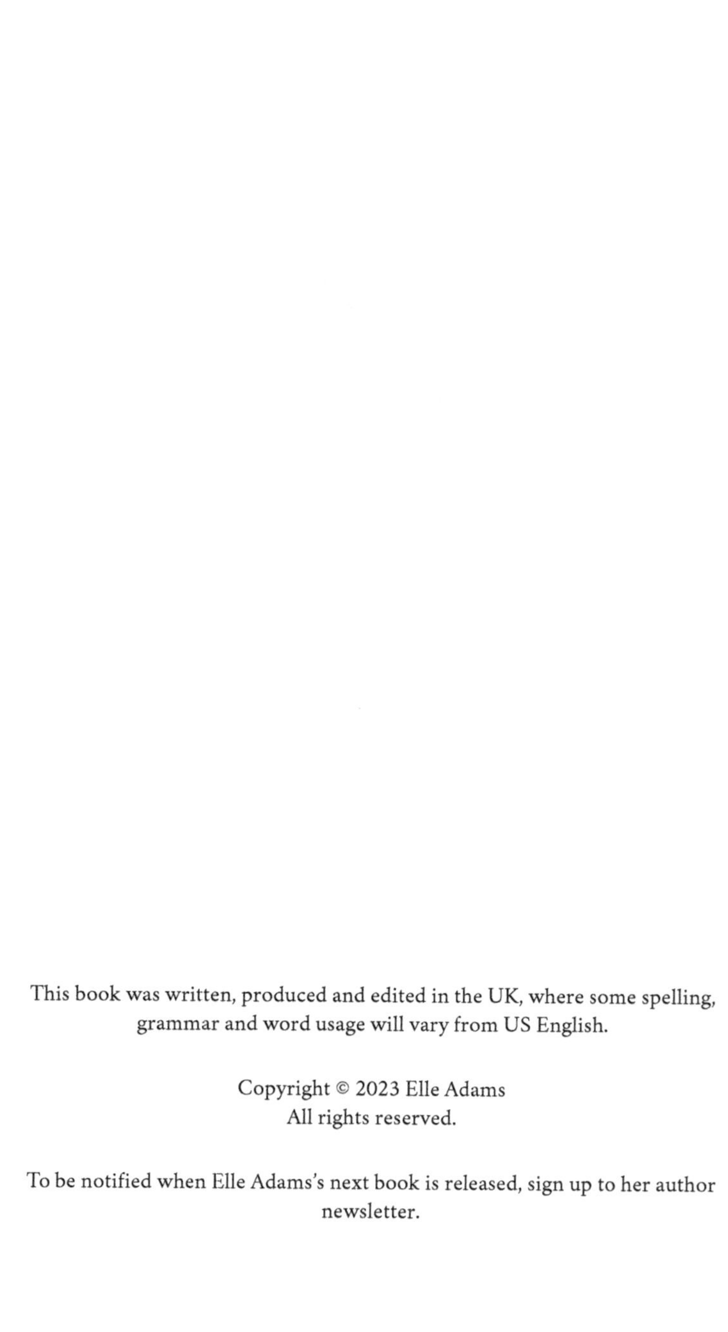

My last day at my dream job didn't exactly get off to a flying start.

Well, technically, I *was* flying—or rather, floating—my feet dangling above my desk as an unseen force levitated me into the air. My coworkers were in a similar state, and Bethan hastily snatched my coffee mug out of the air before it upended itself over my computer. Stacks of paper floated past as Lizzie fiddled with the printer in the corner of our small office.

"Sorry!" she said. "I turned it onto the wrong setting."

She hit a switch, and everyone fell back into their seats. My chair rocked beneath me as I caught my balance against the desk while coffee splashed onto the floor.

"Ack." Bethan, whose pale face was also splattered with coffee, held out the mug to me. "Oops. Sorry, Blair."

"Don't worry about it." I took the now considerably emptier mug from her while she pulled out her wand to clean up the mess. "Lizzie, what was that thing supposed to do?"

"Create a forcefield to keep any hostile forces out of the office." She lifted her head and gave us a sheepish look, accentuated by the ink splattering her dark skin. "I don't think the printer was a fan of the upgrade."

I raised a brow. "Would it work on fairies?"

"I'm not sure," Lizzie said. "Possibly. It's meant to repel anyone who means harm."

"It worked on us," said Rob, who'd somehow managed to keep hold of his coffee mug without spilling any while he'd levitated. The cheerful blond werewolf had been the only person in the office who'd kept doing his job while the rest of us shifted our priorities to survival mode, and I was grateful to him for that.

After all, if the weekend went as I'd planned, I might not be back in my desk on Monday.

At the thought, a ball of anxiety rose inside me. I squished it down with difficulty. I hadn't known what to expect when my coworkers at Dritch & Co had offered to help me in my fight against the Inquisitor, especially when we were supposed to be a paranormal recruitment firm and not an organisation that fought evil. Granted, Dritch & Co was a name that sounded like it ought to apply to both, but our immortal enemy was armed with the most powerful magical item I knew of, and on top of that, he had the help of the entirety of the paranormal hunters. Our small group of three witches and a werewolf seemed a little inadequate in comparison, to say the least.

And the boss, I reminded myself as, in the background, a loud noise arose that sounded like someone trying to coax an ancient car engine to life. Veronica, the boss, had yet to emerge from her office today, but the slightly alarming sounds coming from inside it indicated that she was making preparations of her own.

As if on cue, there came a series of crashes like someone destroying a pile of bricks with a hammer. Or like the local werewolves' band, which played at the New Moon pub every night of the week.

I winced and covered my ears. "If she's planning to destroy the Inquisitor's eardrums, she's on the right track."

"If he's camped outside the town boundaries, it might work," Bethan commented, "but not if he's on the other side of the country."

"I wish," said Lizzie. "Better than thinking about him camping outside town."

"I can't picture him in a tent, can you?" I replied, suppressing a shudder at the reminder of our enemy's close proximity.

"Nah," said Rob. "He's more of the five-star-hotel sort."

"Ha." The amusing image of the fearsome, immortal fairy squatting in a tent didn't quite erase the fact that he was undoubtedly watching like a hawk for any potential chance to slip through our defences and get into Fairy Falls. "I think human accommodation might be a bit plain for him."

As his prime target, I'd asked Veronica if she'd prefer that I keep my distance from the office, but she had replied cheerfully that we were already trapped in the same town together and that it would hardly make a difference if I stayed at home. My coworkers hadn't asked to be dragged into this mess, either, but they'd taken on the role of helping me prepare for the upcoming fight despite my attempts to convince them otherwise.

"Wherever he is, he can't get in, even with that sceptre of his," Bethan said firmly. "That's the important part."

The sceptre's not really his. Clearwater had stolen the artefact from a Head Witch, and I didn't know how he was even able to use it in the first place.

"Speaking of which." Lizzie rose to her feet from next to the printer. "I wish I could have a look at how he got that thing working."

"What? The sceptre?" I asked. "I wish I knew. Aren't they designed for witches only?"

"You'd think," Bethan said from next to me, her hands racing across the keyboard at her usual top speed, "but it's the same for wands, and they can sometimes work when someone who isn't a witch or wizard picks one up. Not very well, mind."

"Then how?" I didn't get it, but the sceptre lent an extra advantage to an enemy who already held all the winning cards. Yes, he was trapped outside of Fairy Falls thanks to a defensive spell Rebecca had cast using her own sceptre, but that didn't mean he'd taken his eyes off of us—or, more specifically, me.

"My mother said that it might be a matter of tradition," she said. "That sceptres choose a witch, I mean. She's been researching."

Another crash from the boss's office accentuated her words.

"When she isn't destroying the property."

"I thought sceptres always chose their wielders," Rob said. "Like Rebecca."

That was true. Rebecca had been picked at the age of eleven, which was much too young to have a major heap of responsibilities piled upon her head, but the sceptre's decision couldn't be challenged. As a result, she'd spent the past few months being dragged from one crisis to another and had inherited a series of enemies who'd have been happy to pry the sceptre from her hands.

It was a bitter irony that just as we had been nearing the point at which we might be able to search for a way to free her of the burden, the enemy had got hold of a sceptre of his own, leaving her as our only real defence against him.

"What does Madame Grey think?" asked Lizzie. "I haven't heard from her in a while."

"She's rushed off her feet, as you might expect," I said. "She thinks Clearwater must have overridden whatever magic makes the sceptre work for only one Head Witch at a time, but even she doesn't know if it's reversible."

"I think our best bet is to get the sceptre away from him," Bethan ventured. "Steal it back and we've taken away his advantage."

"Not counting his own magic."

Fairy magic was powerful in its own right, and Rowe Clearwater's ability to use glamour was unmatched. He'd pretended to be human for years—decades even—and had fooled everyone he met.

Until I'd ripped off his mask for the world to see.

"And his army of fairies," added Rob. "And the hunters too. Do you know if he's taken over just the local branch or the whole country?"

"I wouldn't have thought he'd need to expand outside the region," I replied. "He only took over the hunters so that he had the power to arrest anyone who opposes him. He doesn't want to rule a bunch of humans. I wouldn't have thought he'd have the patience."

It was hard to know with the former Inquisitor, given how far his ruse had gone. Generations of hunters had joined up, not knowing their boss was a fairy—including Nathan, my boyfriend, and his entire family—and a depressing number had remained in their ranks despite the truth coming out.

"He wants power, I thought," said Lizzie. "But I guess it's hard for even him to be in two places at once."

"Exactly."

Didn't stop him from trying, though. Several of Nathan's family members worked for the hunters, and we'd discussed the possibility that the former Inquisitor might make use of their connections to lay a trap for me or both of us. I hated the idea that I might bring his family to harm, but Nathan's brothers had refused all his invitations to come to Fairy Falls instead. Besides, everyone who came into town from the outside had to be vetted in case they had ties to the enemy. It was a necessary rule, but I hated imposing restrictions on the community that had welcomed me into the paranormal world when I hadn't known I was magical at all.

I'd always known, on some level, that it would come to this, not just because the former Inquisitor wanted revenge on me for exposing his identity but because he'd never suffered any real consequences for the crimes he'd committed. He'd been involved in my mother's death. He'd locked up my father and split up my family. He'd even been distantly linked to driving the fairies out of Fairy Falls in the first place.

This was the ideal place to bring an end to him.

Maybe not in the office, though. No matter how many ingenious contraptions Lizzie came up with, I didn't want to put my coworkers in harm's way. Bethan, too, was using her hyper-fast research skills to build lists of potential allies and contact them. As was her mother when she wasn't doing… whatever was responsible for the crashing noises erupting from her office.

I covered my ears again. "What *is* she doing in there? Do you know?"

"Your guess is as good as mine," Bethan answered.

A hissing sound cut through the clamour, drawing my attention to the coffee machine. "Is it supposed to be doing that?"

"Oh, yes, don't worry," Lizzie told me. "It's brewing something special for you."

"It's not a lucky latte, is it?" I asked warily as she began filling a flask. "Not that I don't appreciate it, but I could do without the backlash."

"I thought of that, but no," replied Lizzie. "It's a new concoction I've been working on."

It'd take more than a lucky latte to get us out of this one. The magical beverage tended to backfire once the recipient's luck ran out, and I hoped Lizzie's new creation didn't come with similar side effects.

My gaze then went to the printer, which had gone ominously quiet, which might mean it was plotting revenge for the latest update. We never really knew with that printer. It wasn't sentient in a literal sense, but Lizzie's magic had imbued it with enough of a personality that I was pretty sure it knew we were facing a battle. When I'd come into the office the day after the Inquisitor had delivered his ultimatum, it had spat out a sheet of paper that said, LET'S FIGHT.

I didn't think even the Inquisitor would be deterred if the printer decided to spit brightly coloured ink all over his face, but we needed all the advantages we could get.

When Lizzie finished filling the flask, I realised the noise from the boss's office had stopped. I turned as the door swung inward, and a rather dishevelled Callie came into the office.

"Did you mean to levitate everything in the reception?" asked the werewolf receptionist, who also happened to be Rob's cousin. "Including me?"

"Oops," said Lizzie. "My mistake."

"Please tell me it didn't hit the boss as well."

Uh-oh. That might have explained the volume of the noise.

"I don't know," said Callie, pushing a handful of tangled

blond hair from her face, "but she wants to speak to you, Blair."

My heart gave a familiar lurch, though it was a bit ridiculous to worry about being in trouble with the boss when Veronica had volunteered to help me defend the town against evil. She wasn't going to kick me out at this point, was she? Besides, I'd told her myself that I might not come back to work on Monday, no matter how this weekend went.

Callie led the way out of the small office and through the reception area and knocked on the door at the back.

"Come in, Blair," said Veronica.

Through the boss's open door, I glimpsed... "Is that a cannon?"

"Isn't it great?"

She beckoned me inside, and I dubiously stepped into a room that looked like it was set up for a siege. The walls appeared to be reinforced with metal and covered in spikes. I stepped forward tentatively, wary of the cannon that sat beside the desk, pointing directly at the door.

Seeing my hesitation, my boss beckoned to me again. "Relax, Blair. It won't harm you. It's set to react only to threats."

Knowing my boss, that wasn't entirely reassuring. Keeping half my attention on the cannon, I found a chair amid the chaos and sat down. "Erm, Lizzie's spell didn't levitate everything in here, too, did it?"

"Yes, but it was a good chance for me to test the defences." She indicated a cannonball-shaped dent in the back of the door.

I surreptitiously inched my seat away from the mouth of the cannon. "Good. I think."

Honestly, it probably said something about the general atmosphere at Dritch & Co that a cannon firing at the door wasn't the weirdest thing I'd encountered here. When I'd first moved to Fairy Falls and had shown up at work with no clue that I'd walked into the magical world, Dritch & Co had set the tone for my experience in the magical world at large. At this point, nothing surprised me.

"How are the preparations going?" asked Veronica. "Well?"

"I think so." I moved the chair again when the cannon swerved to follow my motion. "Were you planning to use that on the Inquisitor?"

"If he comes in here," she answered.

"That's not likely, is it?" I asked warily. "I mean, he can't get into Fairy Falls."

Thanks to Rebecca. A sealing spell cast by a sceptre was the only thing that could keep him out, but it was unfortunate that the sceptre in question was in the hands of an eleven-year-old girl.

"No, but I think we should be prepared for any scenario," she said. "That's what Madame Grey told me, and she does tend to have a knack for understanding these situations, doesn't she?"

"Yeah, she does."

I wouldn't have put it past the former Inquisitor to try to trick his way into the town, though we'd taken steps to make sure he wouldn't find it as easy as putting on a glamour. There was only so much we could do, though, and Clearwater's skills were stronger than those of anyone else I'd known. Not that I knew *that* many fairies, but he must have been unique among them to have fooled everyone into thinking he was human for so long. Despite Fairy Falls's name, the fairies had only recently begun to make their return after being driven out, and as a result, I'd had entirely too little experience with fairy magic myself despite my dad's best efforts to teach me.

"In any case," Veronica went on, "I wanted to ask how you were doing, Blair."

"Erm. Fine." There was no adequate way to describe the mixture of terror and determination that drove me onward as more time passed without Clearwater making a direct attack. "I'm not yet sure if we'll be going away this weekend, but my dad will let me know tonight."

By "away," I meant "to the realm of the fairies," not the same realm which Rowe Clearwater had once ruled over but a different one. The place where my dad had once lived before he'd moved to the human realm and fallen in love with my mother.

"I see," she said. "You don't think you'll be back for work on Monday?"

"I hope I will, but my dad told me that time in the fairy realm tends to get a little… weird." According to him, whole days could pass in the space of an hour, and there was no telling how long it might take to find my fairy relatives and attempt to convince them to help us. For the same reason, he didn't know how long had passed in fairy years since his last visit. It might have been days. Or decades.

"I see," she said. "In that case, I wish you the best of luck. I'll ask the others to continue their preparations."

"Thanks." I gave the cannon a wary look. "Have you had much luck finding other allies? Or is that what Madame Grey's doing?"

"I believe Madame Grey has been warning the covens of the former Inquisitor's threat to their safety," she said, her tone uncharacteristically grave. "There's no telling if he'll strike against them out of anger at not having access to Fairy Falls, but they've come up with some quite ingenious ways of protecting themselves."

"Good." Guilt writhed inside me. If Clearwater attacked another paranormal community in a fit of rage at not being able to access this one, it would be hard not to feel partly responsible. "I hope I can find allies in the fairies' realm, but..."

But realistically, I'd be lucky to get out without being bespelled or worse. The fairies weren't known for their fondness for humans, and in some of their eyes, my dad had betrayed them to be with my mother, not just because she was human but because the original Wildflower Coven had helped the Inquisitor drive the fairies out of the area in the first place. My mother hadn't shared the opinions of her ancestors, and neither did I, but that didn't mean the fairies would be inclined to hear me out.

"I'm sure you will," said Veronica. "In the meantime, I'll continue my search for the coven that created the sceptres."

I looked up in surprise, almost falling out of my seat when the cannon reacted to the movement by pointing itself directly at my head. "Ah! You're looking for..."

"The sceptres' creators, yes," she said. "I believe that turning that instrument against the former Inquisitor will take away some of his advantage."

"Do you think they can be found?" Not even Madame Grey knew how the sceptres had been created originally, or so I thought. "Are they like the wand-makers? A coven with a gift nobody else has that created the sceptres?"

"Yes, but no new sceptres have been created for many centuries, to my knowledge," she said. "They're likely to be long dead."

My heart sank. "But you're looking for them anyway?"

"That's right." She gave me a smile. "I'm good at finding people. I found you, didn't I?"

I didn't even know what to say to that, but as her smile implied dismissal, I rose to my feet. As I did so, the cannon levelled itself at my face.

"Ah, nice cannon. Very nice." *Please don't fire at me.*

"Isn't it?" She gave me a little wave as I backed towards the door. At least I could count on one thing amid all the chaos: my boss's ability to be utterly unpredictable.

And she was right. She *had* found me back when I'd been living in the normal world with no idea that I was anything more. If anyone could find a long-dead coven, too, it was Veronica Eldritch.

2

How was one supposed to prepare for a trip to the fairy realm?

The question danced around my thoughts as I walked home from work, at least until my phone began to buzz in my pocket. I fished it out and found that my foster parents were calling me. *Ack.* How was I supposed to explain all this? "All this" being everything that had happened in the past few weeks and possibly a year of context to back it up.

My foster parents weren't part of the magical world, so I wasn't strictly allowed to tell them anything about it at all. They'd met my dad, but he'd been in his human guise at the time, and they didn't know he was a fairy. Didn't know *I* was half fairy and half witch, either. Yet now that my visit to the fairies' realm loomed overhead, I was hit by a thought: How would I make sure Clearwater didn't take advantage of my absence and target them while I was gone?

The phone continued to buzz, and I took in a breath before answering. "Erm… hi."

"Blair!" said Mrs Wilkes. "How are you?"

"Good." The word rang hollow. "I'm good. Are you?"

"We're doing great!" she gushed. "We haven't seen you in ages."

"Yeah." No need to mention that I was kind of being held hostage in my own home. "I've been busy."

"What about this weekend?" Mrs Wilkes asked. "We're both free. How about we come and visit?"

"Ah, Dad and I are going on a trip," I said, which was technically true. "We'll be gone for a few days, but I'd love to see you when we're back."

"Oh, of course!" she said. "I hope you have a lovely time. Where are you going?"

"Erm..." *Think of a name, Blair.* "Another small village north of the lake. You won't have heard of it."

Mostly because Fairyland didn't appear on any maps. Neither did Fairy Falls itself, for that matter, which was one reason they hadn't visited, aside from the obvious. We always met up in Sloan, the neighbouring town, which was a normal community without any magic in sight.

"Anyway, I'm going to visit him now," I said, which was also true. "Talk to you soon?"

"Yes, of course, Blair," she said. "Have an amazing time! Love you!"

I heard Mr Wilkes shouting the same words in the background, and my chest tightened. They didn't know how much danger they might be in simply due to proximity to me —and to the magical world in general. I needed to tell them the truth or some version of it, but I hadn't the faintest idea where to begin. Magic aside, they were thrilled for the new life I'd built. I hadn't the heart to ruin that image for them.

My foster parents had done their best for me, but I'd always felt out of step with other kids my age and with people in general. It was only when I'd discovered the magical world and my own unique family history that all the missing pieces had slotted into place. Now? I was adrift once again, and even the flat that Alissa and I had shared for more than a year made me feel as if I was trespassing in someone else's life. I'd cleaned up the mess after Aveline Hollyhock had vacated my room, but being able to sleep under my own roof for the first time in ages didn't make me any less conscious that I'd unintentionally brought danger upon everyone in my life through my feud with Rowe Clearwater.

As for my foster parents…

"I should send someone to watch them," I muttered to myself. "Someone who doesn't mind leaving the safety of Fairy Falls. Which isn't many people. Is anyone likely to volunteer?"

"Miaow," answered my cat, the only other person in the room. Sky had commandeered the sofa, pushing off Alissa's cat, Roald, and forcing him to retreat into Alissa's room. How the little black cat managed to take up enough space for three people was a mystery that only experts on fairy cats held the answer to, and I was certainly no expert.

"Miaow yourself," I replied absentmindedly. "I don't suppose you know any people willing to volunteer to guard a couple of normals without giving away that the paranormal world exists?"

Sky jumped off the sofa and padded over to me before lifting his front paw into the air. "Miaow."

"What does that mean?" I looked into his eyes—one grey, one blue. "Are *you* offering to guard them?"

He lifted his paw again. "Miaow."

"Are you sure?"

I didn't know how I felt about sending my cat into potential danger while I was gone, but Sky could take care of himself. He might have looked small and unassuming, but as a fairy cat, he could glamour himself to look like a giant. While that wouldn't scare off Clearwater, it might make him think twice about meddling with my foster parents.

"If you want to watch them while I'm in the fairy realm, I don't know how long I'll be gone." I petted him, and Sky purred and arched into my hand.

"Yes, I know we've been planning this for a while," I added, as if I was having a conversation with someone who could talk back with words other than "miaow." "But it's dangerous, and I don't know what to expect of the fairies. Even if they are family, technically."

"Miaow." Sky butted his head into my palm.

"What?" I lifted my hand. "Yes, I know I don't need any more family members than the ones I've already got, but we need their help. I'd like to think Dad's relatives would care about Clearwater threatening him, but I don't know how they'll react to *me*."

The fairies played by different rules than the rest of us did. Who knew what they'd think of me, the half-fairy offspring of someone who'd once been a prince of one of their realms? That had been a long time ago, though, and Dad had said himself that his old home might be unrecognisable after such an extensive absence.

Sky butted my hand again, more aggressively.

"Yes, I know I need to go to see my dad and ask if he's managed to get in touch with them." I gave him one last stroke and rose to my feet. "Are you coming with me?"

Sky yawned, padded back to the sofa, and curled up for a nap.

That's a no, then.

I quickly changed out of my work clothes and into something more casual before leaving for my dad's house. Pretty much all the streets in Fairy Falls led to the woods eventually, but I stuck to the quieter areas to avoid drawing too much attention. The stares were kind of unavoidable, given that I was the chief reason the town was now encased in a magical bubble that nobody could leave without risking being targeted by an evil fairy, but that didn't mean I *liked* being gawked at.

Some of the tension lifted from my shoulders as I entered the forest and the human noise faded into the background, enabling me to hear the rush of the waterfall that gave Fairy Falls its name. Warm sunlight spilled through gaps in the trees, a reminder that with the improved weather came summer. In fact, we were close to the solstice, which would mark a year since my first failed attempt to see my dad when he was in jail.

So much had changed since then. For all of us.

I slowed my pace as my vision flickered, and shimmering light revealed the path that led to the part of the forest the fairies had settled in. Only those of us with the ability to see through glamour could see the way in and out, and I snapped my fingers to bring out my fairy wings as I flew into the brightness. The world gained an evanescent glow, and the sound of the waterfall dimmed as I entered the fairies' home.

Would the *actual* fairy realm be the same? I assumed so, but this was a bubble universe created by glamour less than a year ago, not one of the ancient realms in which fairies had existed since centuries before I was born. According to my dad, the fairies owned countless realms, or courts, and each was ruled by a different family. That was the reason he'd had so much trouble figuring out how to get into contact with his former home without alerting the other courts and specifically Rowe Clearwater. If Clearwater found my dad's family, I didn't know what would happen, but it wouldn't be good.

At the end of the path lay a clearing. I slowed, seeing a few dozen fairies clustered outside the stone houses, talking amongst themselves. These included my friends Rosalyn and Ani, but Conor was there, too, and even Oak, who I'd thought had shunned all human contact. And, of course, my dad. His long hair was far silkier than mine, and his ears were pointed, but our features were recognisably similar, enough that his fairy relatives would have no doubt that we were related.

I felt myself flush as all the fairies' attention turned towards me when I approached. "Ah—what's going on, Dad?"

"We're having a meeting," he explained. "Or we were, anyway. We're just wrapping things up."

"Oh?" Wary, I scanned the crowd. "What about? Fighting him—the former Inquisitor?"

"Fighting Clearwater, yes."

Several fairies flinched at the name, including Ani. She must have taken the evening off work because she was usually assisting Samuel, the vampire who worked in the library at the university. It was a point of pride that I'd got her the job, but not all the fairies had settled into life quite that easily, like Oak and Conor, who barely left their houses. But these days, I didn't really blame them, and my dad must have worked hard to persuade them to come to this meeting.

"We're preparing for the possibility that he might try to access Fairy Falls through here," Rosalyn said in a tremulous voice. "Through our part of the woods, I mean. We're not covered by the shielding spell."

"He'd have to go into Fairy Falls itself to find the way in, remember?" It was a loophole I'd been proud of; as long as Clearwater couldn't pass by the boundaries surrounding Fairy Falls, he couldn't get into the fairies' home, either. Rebecca's shielding spell had only covered the physical boundary around the outskirts of the town, not the bubble universe within created entirely from the fairies' glamour, but even Clearwater couldn't teleport directly into the fairies' home without passing through the boundary spell.

"I wouldn't put it past him to try," said Dad. "I don't expect that we're his priority, but we're definitely on his list of targets."

"That's why we need to move," Conor said with an edge to his voice that made me tense.

He and my dad might have been close friends, but I'd always been a little wary around him, mostly because of that one time he'd almost hit me with a magical lightning bolt. Really, anyone would have been wary after that.

"Before he finds a way in."

"Move where?" I queried. "If you move the entrance to your part of the forest, you might not be able to escape if he does find the way into Fairy Falls. Last time, even I couldn't get in to warn you."

It'd scared me half to death, thinking my dad was gone and that I couldn't get back to him. I never wanted to experience that again.

"I know." Dad's voice softened. "I know, and that's why I think our backup should be to move into Fairy Falls itself."

"What—you want to move into the forest?" The elves and the werewolves would not be fans of that, but if it came to it, they'd help the fairies fend off Clearwater's forces. They'd done it before. "Or the town itself?"

"Potentially, yes," he replied. "We're still talking about our options."

Conor wore a scowl that suggested the notion of moving into a house within reach of the general population was as appealing as diving into the lake in winter. He did technically live next door to the regular people, but he'd hidden his house with glamour so thoroughly that nobody had been able to find him for years except my dad and, later, me.

Oak looked even less thrilled at the idea than Conor did. A former exile like him wouldn't want to entrust his safety to the humans who'd descended from those who'd originally driven him out of town.

"It might not happen, though," I added. "Right?"

"It might not," Dad agreed. "In any case, I think we're done here, aren't we?"

A murmur of agreement passed among the fairies, and some of them began to leave the clearing. Oak was the first to go, vanishing in a dramatic sweep of glittering light.

"That guy will have to be dragged kicking and screaming out of his house if you do decide to move," I muttered to my dad. "No way will he consent to living amongst humans."

"I expect not." He lifted his hand in farewell as Conor left the clearing too. "That's a last resort, though. Besides, he's not one of Clearwater's prime targets."

While the fairies dispersed, Dad beckoned me into his house. I followed, happy to get away from the stares, and was not the least bit surprised to find Sky the cat had fallen asleep on Dad's sofa in more or less the same position I'd left him in at my own flat. As a fairy cat, he could effortlessly move around in ways that were off-limits to regular people and animals. Lucky for him.

I squeezed myself into a space on the sofa that Sky hadn't claimed and gave him a stroke.

"I have some good news," my dad said, closing the door behind him. "My message got through. I've been in touch with my former court."

My heart jumped into my throat. "Really?"

"Yes." He joined me, taking a seat in an armchair. "I managed to secure us permission to visit."

"Meaning, I can go with you?" Questions exploded in my mind. "I thought... I mean, are you sure I'll be welcome there?"

"I can't make any guarantees, but I'll keep you safe."

My mouth went dry. The Court of Eventide had once been my dad's home—in fact, he'd been its ruler—so he could expect some degree of respect despite some of the fairies' opposition to his union with my mother. Me, though? I was a nobody human and entirely too vulnerable to their magic despite being half fairy myself. I scarcely knew the rules for surviving in the fairies' realm except to avoid drinking goblin brew. Or anything, for that matter. The whole realm was laced with enchantments designed to ensnare unwary humans, and they had no reason to be nicer to me than to any other humans who stepped into their midst.

My dad's concerned expression deepened. "Unless you want to stay behind?"

"No." I couldn't let my dad go there alone. "But they won't turn out to be on Clearwater's side, will they?"

"No," he said. "Trust me, they won't be. Most fairies won't approve of what he did."

I hoped he was right, but that didn't bode well for whether they'd approve of what my dad had done, either. Out of their hatred for the covens, some of the local fairies had even gone as far as to support the hunters instead.

I took in a breath. "Are we going tomorrow? I told my boss I might be gone for a few days."

"Good idea," he said. "She seems quite adaptable, but it's better to give her prior warning."

"Or eccentric." I smiled wryly. "She has a cannon in her office in case Clearwater walks in."

"A *cannon?*"

"A magical one, I think." I gave Sky another stroke, conscious that I needed to check in with a lot of other people before I went to the fairy realm. "I haven't had the chance to tell Madame Grey yet. I should drop in at the witches' head-quarters before I go home."

I expected at least one objection—either from Nathan or from Rebecca—when I told them the news, but it wouldn't do much good to put off the decision. After Dad and I had chatted a bit more, I reluctantly got to my feet.

Dad eyed my cat. "He's not coming with us, is he?"

"No. He volunteered to watch my foster parents, actually." I gave Sky a last pet. "Figured someone ought to keep an eye on them while we're gone."

"Oh." He inclined his head. "I didn't think of that. Clearwater has left them alone so far."

"But we don't know how long we'll be gone," I reminded him. "I figured I should take precautions. They aren't in Fairy Falls, after all."

Pretty much everyone else I cared about was here, behind the barriers of the spell Rebecca had cast—but when my dad and I went into the fairies' realm, we'd intentionally be leaving the safety of the town behind.

I hope it's worth it.

I walked past rows of vibrant flowers and returned to the path through the forest, savouring the moments of quiet. Once I left the fairies' realm behind, my wariness returned, and I scanned every bush in case of an ambush. The elves' king had been asking questions about my impending trip, too, but I didn't have time to pay him a visit, and I was relieved when the elves didn't waylay me on my way out of the forest.

I made for the witches' headquarters first, entering the grand house to find that the door to the classroom where I usually had my magic lessons was slightly ajar. Inside, Rebecca sat talking to Rita, our instructor. The tween Head Witch must have had a private lesson that I hadn't been invited to, but I didn't mind. She needed all the help she could get to master the sceptre—or at least prevent her awful mother from getting her hands on it—and it didn't entirely surprise me to find Madame Grey in the room too.

"Blair." Madame Grey nodded to me from beside the desk. Dressed in her usual sweeping grey robes, she looked like a cross between a stylish grandmother and the supreme ruler of the universe. Her silver hair was expertly styled, and her glasses reflected the violet light from the end of the sceptre Rebecca clutched in both hands.

"Hey," Rebecca said to me. "I didn't know you were coming."

"I'm not here for a lesson," I clarified. "I just wanted to tell you—all three of you—that my dad's family said yes. I'm going to meet them tomorrow."

My heart jangled in my throat, especially when I saw the panic in Rebecca's eyes. "What?" she squeaked. "You're going to the fairies' realm? I thought it was lethal for humans."

"I'll be with my dad," I said. "Don't worry. He said it'll be fine."

"I see," said Madame Grey with a glance at Rita. "You're sure that's what you want to do?"

The other witch—red-haired, middle-aged, and with her arms decorated with enough bangles to form a musical chorus whenever she moved—looked almost as concerned as Rebecca did. "I imagine she is, right, Blair?"

I inclined my head. "Yeah. My dad used to be in charge there, even if it was a long time ago, and I—and I think I ought to go with him."

"You've got to be joking."

The snide remark came from Blythe, who stepped into view from the other side of the door I'd left ajar. "You think you can persuade them? They'll eat you alive."

"Someone has to try."

I should have guessed she'd be lurking around to spy on her sister's lessons. Blythe and I had never been friendly—not least because our families had been mortal enemies—and while she'd mellowed a little after her mother had been jailed, worry for her sister made her prone to snapping at anyone she thought was putting Rebecca at risk. Which was usually me.

"What does it matter to you?" I asked her.

"If you get kidnapped or worse, you know what'll happen here," she said. "Clearwater will think there's nobody standing between him and my sister."

My brows shot up. "Nobody? You think he views me as that much of a threat?"

I never knew what to make of Blythe these days, but that had almost been a compliment. I had my doubts that I presented any real threat to an immortal fairy with an army at his command and a sceptre in his hands—not to mention his alliance with Blythe and Rebecca's mother, who was a powerful witch in her own right.

"No," she said. "You're his main target, though, and once you're gone, he and his entire army will come down on Rebecca instead."

"Not if they can't get in." I glanced at her sister, who'd gone pale. "The town is protected."

"We have to keep redoing the boundary spell," Blythe said. "If you aren't back before we next need to redo the defences, what then?"

"I will be." I didn't intend to spend *that* long in the fairy realm. "The fairies are worried he might find a way to get into their home. They were discussing potentially moving into the town instead of the forest."

"No way," Blythe said with a sharp look at Madame Grey. "We think—"

"You think what?" I swivelled to Madame Grey myself, whose lips were compressed. "What?"

Blythe didn't answer. To say she had trust issues was like saying werewolves were a little hairy. I understood why— she'd been raised by a woman who'd tried to poison her against the covens and who'd terrorised her younger sister— but if we wanted to win this, and if we wanted to keep Mrs Dailey from claiming Rebecca again, we had to share every-thing with one another.

"What is it?" I pressed. "Why isn't it a good idea for the fairies to move out of their part of the woods?"

"Aside from the fact that half of them don't know how phones work?" Blythe said caustically.

Madame Grey cleared her throat. "There's the possibility that Clearwater's next target will be the regional witch council."

My heart jumped. "The local one? He wants more sceptres?"

"Worse."

"What can possibly be worse?" Then I remembered how I'd unmasked him. "Not the Seeing Stone?"

The Seeing Stone. The most powerful magical object I knew of, which would enable Clearwater to have total control over any fairy who crossed his path. If he did get his hands on it, and if the fairies left the sanctuary of the forest, they'd be prime targets.

"That's right," said Madame Grey. "I'm not entirely sure if it's his current priority, but he almost certainly wants it for his own."

Of course he does. The Seeing Stone was currently in the hands of the regional witch council, who used it to see into the future without the need to employ a Seer. My dad had taken it away from the witches to prevent Clearwater from getting his hands on it once before and had endured years in prison as punishment. It'd completely slipped my mind that Clearwater might try the same thing again.

"But where is it?" I asked. "With the council?"

"In one of their houses and under close watch," she said. "That hasn't been known to stop him in the past, however."

No kidding. "Can't we bring it here? To Fairy Falls?"

"That would require some of us to go out in the open," she replied. "And that's a risk in its own right, depending on how many of his people are waiting for us to leave so they can strike."

"Good point." My heart raced. "What can I do?"

"Leave that to us," Madame Grey said. "We'll figure it out. You, Blair… you should focus on the fairies. If you're certain you want to talk to them yourself."

"I am." Not just because they were my long-lost relatives but because they might be our last hope to stop Clearwater.

Whether even *they* could stand against the Seeing Stone, though, remained to be seen.

3

An hour later, I sat at a table in the Troll's Tavern with Nathan beside me and his sister and her fiancé occupying the seats opposite ours. We'd got into the habit of going on double dates once a week, and the sound of chatter and the smell of pub food soothed my frazzled nerves, even if I hadn't exactly come with good news.

Nathan and Erin both knew that I'd been planning to go with my dad to see the fairies, though they weren't particularly happy with the idea, but to my surprise, it was Buck who put his foot down.

"Don't the fairies want to kill you?" he asked.

"Not those fairies," I reminded him. "They're my dad's family, and I'm pretty sure they don't even know I exist."

Buck was half fairy like me, and he knew the difficulty of being caught between two worlds. The other side of his family were normals, though, and the hunters had given him his initial education on the paranormal world itself. He hadn't known until he met me that there was a way to learn about magic that didn't involve joining their ranks.

"Because your dad broke contact with them when he left."

Concern filled his green eyes, which were too bright to belong to a human even when he was wearing glamour that smoothed out his pointed ears. "You told us that. What if they lock you up or worse?"

"My dad is convinced that they won't," I said. "And I trust him. Don't forget he used to rule over their entire court."

"That's a casual way to say he was a *prince.*" Erin leaned across the table, her dark hair falling into curtains on either side of her face. She was already on her third beer, and it wasn't even eight o'clock yet. "I don't envy you having to navigate that mess. Aren't the fairies all centuries old too?"

"Well, yes." I was aware of how absurd it sounded, talking about my dad as a fairy prince—even one who'd given up his crown years ago. "Speaking of family, have any of you managed to get hold of Eric yet?"

Tension rippled up and down the table at the change of subject, but I genuinely wanted to know.

Beside me, Nathan spoke first. "Erin did."

"Eventually." Her mouth curved in a deep scowl. "We argued. I also argued with Jay. I'm all about burning bridges today."

No wonder she was halfway drunk already. "That bad?"

Nathan's family, with the exception of Erin, were ensnared so deeply in the hunters' ranks that they'd refused to leave even when the former Inquisitor had been unmasked. His dad had once run the local hunters' branch, and upon his retirement, that role had passed to Nathan's older brother, Jay. Erin's twin, Eric, was equally committed, and they'd been concerned that he hadn't been answering their calls after the former Inquisitor's return.

"No surprise," Nathan said. "My dad said I was being ridiculous even suggesting that he needed to be warned about the Inquisitor, and Eric parrots everything he says."

"He knows who the Inquisitor really is, though," I said.

"He saw the truth. Helped me figure it out, even. How can he have forgotten?"

"He said he didn't believe it's possible for the Inquisitor to resume control," said Nathan. "He thinks the hunters would reject him."

My hands clenched. "Did you remind him that Clearwater has the ability to use glamour to manipulate people into thinking he's someone else or just outright bewitching them into following him without question?"

"I tried," he said. "But he's flat-out refusing to come into Fairy Falls, and Erin had even less luck with the others."

Erin snorted. "Eric's been offered a promotion. That's why he was so stubborn."

I blinked. "Seriously?"

"Yeah. He's been recruited to join the LFPF." She picked up her beer again. "Jay encouraged him to take the position, the scumbag."

My mouth went dry. "Recruited by whom?"

"He didn't say, but I'm sure we all know who it was." Erin drained her glass.

I stared at her then at Nathan. "He spoke *directly* to Eric? Clearwater did?"

"You know what Eric's like," said Erin. "He was given a special mission by the Inquisitor himself. In his eyes, that's the best honour he could have been given, and he won't give it up for anything."

"Was he asleep when the Inquisitor was unmasked as a fairy?" I dropped my voice when some people glanced towards our table. "When he tried to have us killed?"

"I assume glamour was involved," Nathan put in. "Eric's own hero-worshipping of the man would mean Clearwater wouldn't have had to try that hard."

He's gone too far. Nathan and Erin might not get on with their other family members, but I knew better than to think the former Inquisitor had promoted Eric on his own merits. He'd wanted him close for a reason: as a warning both to Nathan and to me.

"Anyway, forget our ridiculous family," said Erin, tapping her fingertip to the menu to order another beer. "What about yours? Do you think the fairies will help you out?"

"It's a last resort," I admitted. "But they're not fans of Clearwater, and let's face it, we're in need of powerful allies."

"What does Madame Grey think?" asked Nathan.

"She understands my choice," I said. "The problem is, well, she thinks Clearwater is being quiet because his attention is on the regional witch council. They might be his next targets."

"Why would he go after them?" asked Buck.

"Because they have the Seeing Stone."

Alarm flickered across Nathan's face. "He wants the Seeing Stone, of course."

"Come again?" asked Erin. "Why does he want to see the future?"

"It's not just a crystal ball," I whispered. "It also enables him to control anyone who crosses him. Any fairy. It's the reason my dad went to jail. Remember?"

An uneasy silence followed. Everyone remembered the moment I'd unmasked the former Inquisitor, using the Seeing Stone itself to burn away the glamour hiding his true identity. If I hadn't stopped him, he'd have used the stone to dominate the witches *and* the fairies. I'd thought we'd won that day, but I should have known he hadn't given up on his goal. If Madame Grey thought the Seeing Stone was a likely target—and she was rarely wrong—what better time to make his move than when my dad and I were out of reach?

"You can't let that put you off," Nathan finally said. "He might be bluffing, and he might be trying to stop you from getting help. The witches know what they're doing, don't they?"

I looked at him in surprise. "You think I should go to the fairy realm? I expected you to object."

"Of course I don't *like* the idea," he said, "but you're right, someone has to stop Clearwater, and I'll be honest, I'm not sure the answers are here. In this world, I mean."

"They're in the fairies' realm instead." I suspected the same, as much as I wanted to avoid getting my hopes up. "No pressure, then?"

———

The following morning, I woke at dawn to the sound of a pixie tapping on the window of my flat. I stifled a yawn behind my hand. "Right, right, I'm coming."

The pixie flew out of sight of the window while I fumbled to find my clothes. As usual, Sky had hidden all my socks under the bed, as he did whenever he didn't want me to go somewhere.

"Really, Sky?" I extended a hand under the bed, towards the fluffy cat-shaped lump, and got myself clawed for my trouble. "This is how you want to say goodbye?"

"Miaow."

Sky turned his back and sulked while I got dressed, but he came out to rub against my legs as I left my bedroom.

My phone was jammed with "good luck" messages, including several from Nathan. I'd wanted to stay over at his house, but we'd parted ways last night with the understanding that it would be easier on both of us if I left without a prolonged goodbye.

Besides, part of me had expected the pixie to show up. I still hadn't checked in with the elves yet.

When I left my room, I found I wasn't the only one

awake. Alissa stood in the doorway of her bedroom, wrapped in a pink dressing gown. "You're leaving now?"

"I think the elves want me to take a detour first," I replied, catching sight of a flask in her hands. "What's that?"

"For you." She passed it to me. "Bethan gave it to me. Said it's from Lizzie."

"From work?" I took the flask and sniffed the dark liquid inside. "She said she was brewing something for me, but she wouldn't tell me what it was."

"Bethan told me it's for courage."

I sniffed the liquid again, smelling a herbal concoction, but nothing I recognised. "Not alcohol?"

"Nope, but she said to drink one cup before you leave."

"Guess I need all the courage I can get." I tipped out some of the liquid into the flask's cup-shaped lid and drank. Wakefulness flowed through my body, washing away my tiredness and banishing a fair few of my misgivings too. My spine straightened, and I stood taller. "Here's hoping it'll be enough for me to handle the fairies."

"I hope so, too." She hugged me. "I'll see you later?"

"Of course." I left the flask in the kitchen and grabbed my Seven Millimetre Boots. While I didn't necessarily need to use them to fly, they'd be useful if I found myself trapped in a sticky situation. My dad had warned me that it was possible the fairies would try to stop me from accessing my powers, and I wouldn't be able to use my wand in their realm, either. If they blocked my fairy magic, too, I'd be completely at their mercy.

Okay, now I get why Lizzie thought I'd need a shot of courage.

When I left the flat, I found our upstairs neighbour, Nina, peering down from the top of the staircase in the corridor. "I heard you're leaving, Blair."

"Not for long," I told her. "I'm just going to see my dad."

"And the fairies." Her eyes were round. "Alissa told me. Are you sure you're going to be okay?"

"Of course," I said. "I'll be back before you know it."

As I left the building and closed the door behind me, I saw Alissa watching me through the window of our flat, a similar nervous expression on her face.

"Why is everyone acting like I'm going to the gallows?" I addressed my familiar, who'd joined me on the garden path.

"Miaow." Sky padded ahead of me.

I wondered where he was going for a brief instant before I remembered he'd volunteered to go and guard my foster parents while I was gone. I wished I'd asked someone else instead so I could bring him with me, but it was too late for that now.

"Miaow." Sky waited for me at the gate, rubbed against my legs, and then vanished.

"Goodbye to you too," I said to the empty air. I guessed he didn't want to drag our goodbyes out either.

I walked through the centre of Fairy Falls, following the pixie's lead. The small, pointy-eared creature chittered in a language I couldn't understand, flitting up and down and showering the ground with pink glitter. I expected him to lead me deeper into the woods to the elves' home, but instead, he flew straight through to the lake's edge, where a sloping path led to the waterfall.

I halted at the top of the hill. "Wait. I thought we were going to see the elves."

The pixie made one of his chittering noises and then flew downhill. The waterfall came into view as I descended the path, a ceaseless current of water splashing up white foam. *Beautiful.* The Fairy Falls had captivated me since before I'd known I *was* a fairy, and the mere touch of the water stripped off my glamour, allowing me to stretch my wings.

Then I saw the little cat waiting for me on the bank and did a double-take. "Sky?"

No, that wasn't Sky. The cat had the same oddly coloured eyes Sky did, but his paws were all black, whereas a single white paw distinguished my familiar from the other fairy cats.

"Miaow," said the cat.

"You're one of his friends," I surmised. "One of the other fairy cats."

"Miaow." He stepped up to my side and rubbed against my leg.

"You want to come with me?" I guessed.

"Miaow."

Okay. At least I had backup in addition to my dad, but I didn't get why the pixie had dragged me out here instead of sending the cat to my house instead. Unless he'd thought Sky would get jealous.

Hearing a rustling sound, I turned around and saw my dad approaching from farther up the path. "Blair?"

"Hey." I beat my wings, flying up to meet him. "Ready?"

"I was going to ask you the same question, Blair." He eyed the small cat. "You have company."

"Apparently." I held out a hand to stroke the cat, but it shrank out of reach. *Cats. Honestly.* "The pixie showed up at my flat and led me here. Why?"

"Because he knew this was where I intended to cross into my family's home." He indicated the rippling lake below the falls.

"I don't follow." Though now that I thought about it, I hadn't asked him how we were going to actually get from here to the fairies' realm. "Aren't we using a portal?"

Fairy Falls did have one portal, but it led into a different realm than my dad's—to be more specific, it led to the home of Rowe Clearwater. For that reason, we'd sealed the portal against being used, but I didn't know how else we were supposed to get to my dad's former home.

"Anything can be a portal for us, Blair." He flew downwards to the falls, and I followed. "If we have an invitation."

"What invitation?" I'd envisioned something like a wedding invitation, but that was a bit ridiculous when I thought about it. The fairies didn't need a piece of paper to give permission to someone to come to their home, surely.

"This one." He indicated the rippling surface of the lake, where our reflections appeared side by side—along with the cat, which suddenly looked a lot bigger than it had before. Human sized.

"Whoa." Startled, I looked sideways at the little cat, but it remained the same size as usual. Some kind of trick? Or glamour?

"Miaow," the cat said, reaching out a paw to touch the lake's surface and sending ripples spreading outward.

"That's our cue." My dad extended a hand to me.

Bewildered, I let him take my hand and pull me closer to the shore of the lake. "What, the *cat* is our invitation?"

"I haven't done this in a while." Glitter sprang to his fingertips as he lifted his free hand and snapped his fingers. "Don't let go, Blair."

Then he yanked me off my feet and pulled me headfirst into the water. I scarcely had a heartbeat to brace for the soaking—but it never came. Instead, a world of shimmering glitter enveloped me. I stared around, enchanted, until my dad's hand moved in mine, tugging me downward.

Water filtered in. I choked, flailing, legs kicking outwards. The glittering light blurred, and I couldn't see my way to the surface. Unable to breathe, I flailed again—and to my horror, my dad's hand slipped from mine.

Help! I cried out silently, unable to speak without getting a mouthful of water. Something had gone wrong. I kicked and flailed, driving myself upwards—and then Dad's hand gripped mine again.

We surfaced, and I gasped out a breath, relieved and shaken at the same time. "What—what was that?"

"The portal," he said. "Sorry. I should have warned you. You were lucky you let go *after* we got here."

"Got where?" My gaze snapped upwards. While we hovered above the surface of a lake, it wasn't the same one we'd left behind.

Instead of a town, a *castle* sat on a small island off the shore. I didn't have another word to describe the vast building with its turrets, towers, and spiked roofs, but it was bigger than any castle I'd seen at home. Granted, most castles in England were in ruins. This one, though, looked as big as a small town and completely dwarfed its surroundings.

My mouth fell open. "Is that—?"

"That," said Dad, "is the home of the Eventide Court's current ruler."

Oh my god. Shivering, I pulled out my wand to dry myself off.

My dad shook his head. "Remember, you can't use your witch magic here."

"Right." Of course not. This was the realm of the fairies. Not humans. "The Eventide Court won't mind if we show up dripping wet?"

"It'll be fine." He beckoned to me. "As I said, the castle belongs to our family."

Our family. His and mine. Whether that counted for anything remained to be seen.

We flew the short distance to the castle, halting at the edge of a drawbridge.

"If we don't enter through the front doors, we might be taken as intruders," he explained. "Better to do this the official way."

I shivered. "Does the ruler, erm, prince know we're coming?"

"Yes," he said. "She does."

"She?" I echoed. "Who…?"

"My sister, Aster. She goes by the title Lady Eventide."

My heart skipped a beat. His sister. My aunt. "I didn't know."

"She took over as ruler after I moved into the human world," he explained. "She accepted my choice, though she didn't understand it. My parents, less so."

I jumped when the drawbridge lowered before us, as if some unseen person wanted to welcome us to the castle. "We're being allowed in?"

"We did have an invitation, remember?"

"The cat." I spun around, but there was no sign of the small feline. "It isn't still in the lake, is it?"

"Fairy cats are made of strong stuff." He beckoned, taking one step onto the bridge. "Come on, Blair."

On the other side of the drawbridge lay a path to a pair of polished wooden doors. When we reached the doors, they swung inward. Someone was definitely expecting us.

Hoping my courage potion was working to its full extent, I followed my dad into what appeared to be a forest.

I stared around, unprepared for tall trees in place of stone, their branches wreathed in brightness. "Erm, is this supposed to be here?"

"I was afraid of this," he muttered. "My sister is testing me."

"Why?"

"Because she hasn't seen me in years," he said. "Or because she's bored. We're long-lived, Blair, and it's rare that a leader of a fairy realm gets to see this much excitement."

"Then where—?" I broke off as music began to trickle in through the background. The faint, eerie noise wrapped around my body, and my legs began swaying of their own accord. "Oh no."

"Fairy music has a hypnotic effect on humans." He swore under his breath. "I should have expected this too."

"Yeah." I winced when my feet started jerking about underneath me as if they belonged to someone else. "I don't suppose plugging my ears would work?"

"It might."

I hadn't known I'd need to pack earplugs, but I dug in my pockets and unearthed a pack of tissues. Not exactly the safest option if they got stuck, but anything was better than humiliating myself in front of my dad's family and blowing all our chances of recruiting their help against Rowe Clearwater.

As I plugged both ears, brightness dazzled my eyes. The trees were moving inwards, towards us, surrounding us—and when I turned around, the door we'd entered through had disappeared.

"Hey!" I waved my hands, panic threatening to rise. "We're your family. We're not—"

Dad caught my arm, murmuring into my ear. "It's a test for you."

His words were muffled by the tissue, but I got the gist. *Me. They want to test me.*

The trees moved closer. Sharp branches scratched my face, feeling startlingly real for something that was made of—

Glamour.

I raised my right hand, fingers tingling, and reached for the threads I knew made up the illusion. It took several fumbling seconds for me to grasp the edges, reaching beneath the branches to the threads of magic that made them up—and I tugged hard.

The trees collapsed, unfolding one by one as if I'd

knocked over a stack of dominoes. When they'd gone, we stood in an empty hall with stone floors and walls. A cold draught reminded me of my soaking clothes, and I peered up at the balcony overlooking us from the top of a stone stairway.

"Is anyone there?" I called out. "We're here to talk to the ruler of the Court of Eventide. It's about a threat to us—and a threat to you."

"A threat to *my* court, human?" The lilting voice came from above, and its owner fluttered down in front of me in a shower of glittering light.

There was little doubt that this woman was the ruler of the Eventide Court. The crown upon her head was clue enough, but even without it, her elaborately curled hair and the embroidered blue dress she wore screamed royalty.

This was my aunt. Lady Eventide.

4

As I stood before Lady Eventide, it occurred to me that I hadn't asked my dad how one was supposed to greet a monarch of the fairy realm. Was I meant to bow or curtsey? I didn't know, and my wings made it doubly awkward, so I settled for a half crouch with my head bent.

"It's an honour to meet you, Your Majesty." Was that the right form of address? I hadn't a clue, and it didn't help that the slightest mistake might cost me my life or my sanity. When Lady Eventide continued to look upon me without speaking, I remembered the bits of tissue sticking out of my ears and wanted to evaporate on the spot. So much for the potion for courage. Maybe I should have drunk the entire flask instead.

"Isn't she adorable?" She addressed my dad. "What was her name again? Briar?"

"Blair," I said awkwardly. "That's what I'm usually called."

"Briar sounds more appropriate for here," said Lady Eventide. "Wouldn't you say?"

"Erm. If you say so." It wasn't exactly wise to argue with a monarch, especially one whose help I needed. "Absolutely."

"Wonderful." She clapped her hands. "I didn't think I'd see you again here, Braden, but you've surprised me. Won't you both come with me?"

I surreptitiously removed the scraps of tissue from my ears when she turned her back and led the way through a side door off the entrance hall. Beyond lay a sumptuous living room. I followed warily, conscious of the unreal quality that overlaid my vision as if I was seeing the world through tinted glass. Everything screamed luxury, from the flowers on the walls—actual flowers, not wallpaper—to the elaborately carved chairs whose backs were shaped like wolves and foxes.

Lady Eventide snapped her fingers, and a tray of drinks appeared on a low wooden table between the chairs, accompanied by a bowl of fruit. I knew enough from my experience with goblin fruit to avoid both, and Dad and I took two of the smaller chairs. Mine was carved into the likeness of a ferret, while my dad's resembled a large fox.

Lady Eventide claimed the largest chair—or throne, really —which appeared to have been carved out of an entire tree trunk. Branches formed its arms, while roots pushed it upward off the ground so that she towered over the rest of the room.

With a glass in her hand, she smiled down at my dad and me. "Now, what can I do for you?"

"We need your help." My voice sounded pathetically human. It'd seemed easy, in theory, to promise everyone at home that I'd go to see the fairies and convince them to help, but now, the words lodged in my throat, and all my rehearsed pleas seemed laughable. Why would this woman, this fairy, give up all this luxury to fight for the freedom of a town full of humans?

"I gathered," said Lady Eventide. "Tell me more, Briar."

"We're being attacked by another fairy," I blurted. "I don't know how much my dad told you, but he's called Rowe Clearwater."

"Ah, yes, Braden told me that Clearwater is up to some trickery in the human world."

"Worse than trickery." My courage returned as the indignation at everything Clearwater had done overwhelmed me. "He spent decades using glamour to pretend to be human so he could rule over the paranormal hunters, persecuting anyone who crossed him. Now, he's doing the same again, and he's also stolen a powerful wand—a sceptre—from the witches. He has the entire town of Fairy Falls under siege."

"A town, you say?" she asked. "How many people live there?"

"Erm, I don't know. A few hundred." When I said it aloud, our concerns sounded small compared to ruling a kingdom. But Fairy Falls was my whole world, and I didn't know how to put that into words for a stranger who no doubt saw all humans as small and insignificant. "But he has the power to do worse. The hunters have influence over the entire region, and if he takes out the covens, nobody will stand in his way."

She eyed me with one brow slightly arched. "The covens? The same covens who tried to have you arrested? Who drove our kin out of their town?"

Ack. Shouldn't have mentioned them.

"He tried to kill my dad," I said desperately. "He wants us both dead, and he'll get his way unless we can stop him. The sceptre makes him pretty much a one-man army, and he has at least one actual army at his command, too. His fairy allies *and* the hunters outnumber us by a mile. We need help."

"Sceptre," she repeated. "Do the witches not have similar weapons themselves?"

"Well, yes, but not all of them, and there's no defending

against glamour." I dropped my gaze. "Except for fairies, and there are only a handful of us in Fairy Falls."

I intentionally placed myself among the fairies in the hopes of gaining her understanding, but no such luck. Lady Eventide pursed her lips. "I gather that your covens are to blame for that, aren't they?"

"That doesn't mean their descendants deserve to suffer for what our ancestors did," I protested. "It was Clearwater's fault too. He conspired with the old covens centuries ago to drive out any fairy who might oppose him. Now, he's back, and we don't have a big enough army to stand up to him."

Dad shifted in his seat. "I did mention that if he wins, there's a chance he'll come here next, didn't I, Aster?"

"Yes, yes, you did," she said. "But I can hardly bring my army to the human world, can I? Their realm is poisonous to our kind. I never understood why you were so taken with it."

I opened and closed my mouth. I didn't have any argument to that; after all, my dad had gone against custom when he'd moved to the human realm, whereas I'd lived there my whole life.

A meowing noise cut in before my dad could reply, drawing my eyes to the door. The little black cat, which I'd forgotten about, had nudged the door open and walked in. As I watched, perplexed, the cat sprang across the room and climbed up onto Lady Eventide's chair.

Only a cat would have the nerve to drape himself across a throne as if it was a ratty old sofa, but Lady Eventide didn't seem to mind. "I wondered where you'd got to, Bronze."

"He's yours?" So much for him being my backup in this strange world. I almost wished I'd brought Sky, though his own lack of respect for authority might have made her even less inclined to help us.

"That's right," she said. "You have a fairy cat companion of your own, don't you, Blair?"

"Yes, Sky," I said. "But he's guarding my foster parents. They're human, and the Inquisitor is likely to target them as potential hostages. There's little he won't do to harm me—and my dad too. That's why we're so concerned."

"Understandable." She rose upright, and the little cat jumped off her lap. "However, bringing my own people into your realm is out of the question, I'm sorry to say."

My heart sank at the dismissal in her voice, knowing that I was out of arguments.

"I see." Dad stood, beckoning to me. "We'll go. Thank you for your hospitality, and it's good to see you again, Aster."

"Oh, the same to you," she said. "You look well, for a wonder, given how many years you've spent with the humans. All that metal and smoke takes a toll."

"Fairy Falls isn't like that," he said. "It used to be ours, and I believe it can be again if Clearwater isn't allowed to take it back."

"I wish you the best of luck." She offered a smile, and Dad and I left the room with the sense of having avoided a fatal car crash only to drop dead from a poisoned arrow a moment later.

The entrance hall was deserted; for the first time, it struck me as strange that we hadn't seen another person aside from Lady Eventide. Unless the castle's other inhabitants had glamoured themselves invisible, which was entirely possible. Dad didn't stop to look, so I didn't either.

We'd reached the other side of the drawbridge before he spoke. "Don't feel bad, Blair. Getting my sister's help was always a long shot."

My shoulders slumped. "But doesn't she care that you and I might die?"

"Of course she does," he said, "but think about it from her perspective. We might be related, but the other fairies in her court have no loyalty towards me or the human world. Now, if Clearwater showed up *here*, it'd be a different story."

"He might." My hands fisted. "I'm sure he won't stop with our little corner of the human world."

"I know," he said. "However, she doesn't believe the threat to her own people is imminent."

That figured. And to add insult to injury, we had to dive into the lake again to get home. When we approached the edge of the water, my dad took my hand.

"This time, try not to let go," he said. "We should end up in the same place where we left, but you never know with portals."

And on that reassuring note, he tugged me forward, over the edge, and into the lake. Water closed over our heads, darkness beckoning. I held my breath, gripping my dad's hand tight, and let him pull me back to the surface.

As cold air filled my lungs, a voice drifted into my water-logged ears. "Who's that?"

I coughed, struggling to get my bearings, as another voice spoke. "Hey, it's that Blair. What's she doing?"

I shoved a curtain of sopping hair out of my eyes and spied three humans blinking at me from the lakeside. To be specific, three *hunters*, whose real names I didn't know but whom I called Sleepy, Dopey, and Grumpy.

"What are you doing here?" Releasing my dad's hand, I jumped upward, wings spreading into flight. "You shouldn't be able to get into Fairy Falls."

"We're not in Fairy Falls." My dad spoke from behind me in calm tones. "We're outside the border."

I spun around, seeing that we weren't near the waterfall but on the other side of the town's boundaries. *Uh-oh.*

"What *are* you doing in the lake?" asked Sleepy.

"Erm." Crap. I didn't need them to know I'd been visiting the fairies. "Swimming. It's a lovely day."

"You need your wings to swim?" Grumpy asked dubiously.

"Yes." I beat my wings, edging closer to the town's border, but Rebecca's defensive spell might keep even *me* out of the town if nobody was around to confirm I wasn't an intruder. Besides… "Why are you three hanging around here?"

Spying on us, I assumed, perhaps in the hopes that they'd find a way to sneak into town. The hunters didn't answer, but another suspicion arose. "Where is she? Mrs Dailey?"

"None of your concern," said Sleepy.

"That's right," Dopey said. "She's not here."

Grumpy shoved him in the shoulder. "Don't tell her that."

"I'd already worked that out for myself." Mrs Dailey wouldn't have been able to resist showing her face; she was as obsessed with what was going on inside Fairy Falls as the Inquisitor was. Especially concerning her children. "Why you, though? Does she not have anyone better to send to run errands for her?"

"Think you're funny, do you?" said Grumpy.

"Just being honest." I shivered, reminded that this was my second soaking of the day and that I should probably cast a drying charm before I caught a chill.

When I reached for my wand, all three of them tensed, reaching for their own weapons.

"I'm not starting a fight, I'm drying myself off."

"We're not supposed to fight you, anyway." Dopey broke off when Grumpy hit him in the arm.

"Because Mrs Dailey told you not to?" I dried off my clothes with a flick of my wand and surveyed them. "Interesting. Any reason?"

"Yes," said Dopey.

Grumpy hit him again. "Shut *up.*"

"Why *does* Mrs Dailey have you running errands for her?" I pressed. "You'd think she'd have found more competent allies now that she's free from jail and has the rest of the hunters running around, doing her bidding."

"Huh?" said Dopey. "They aren't doing her bidding."

Grumpy grabbed him by the scruff of his neck. "Want me to throw you into the lake?"

I took a step closer to them. "What does that mean? Mrs Dailey doesn't have the hunters' support?"

Had they all taken sides with the former Inquisitor instead? I'd thought he and Mrs Dailey were on the same side, but they were allies by necessity, and Clearwater undoubtedly didn't like the idea of sharing power. *That's interesting.*

"Intruders!" a voice shrieked.

I looked for the source and saw that a mermaid had risen to the surface of the lake and spotted the hunters.

"Intruders!" More merpeople caught the word and echoed it back and forth across the lake.

I caught my dad's eye, and he gave me a slight smile, indicating that he was the one who'd warned them of their unwelcome visitors, but part of me had wanted to keep up the questioning to see what else Dopey inadvertently let slip.

Grumpy released Dopey and glared at the merpeople. "We aren't intruding. See?"

The merpeople continued to shout "intruder" back and forth between themselves, ignoring him. Then a small, pointy-eared figure ran into view, wielding a sharp stick. "Intruders!"

This time, the hunters wisely backed away as several other elves came running up to join the first. Each was around four feet tall, but they far outnumbered the hunters, and those pointy sticks were no joke.

Sleepy, looking more awake than I'd ever seen him, grabbed Dopey's arm and pulled him out of range of the oncoming elves.

"We'll be back, Blair Wilkes!" said Grumpy, sounding like a less impressive version of the Terminator.

As he and the others fled, some of the elves pursued them.

One, a short-tempered elf called Bramble, approached me. "Blair Wilkes. The king would speak to you."

"Now?" I blinked. "I just got back from the fairy realm."

No doubt that was exactly what he wanted to discuss, and sure enough, Bramble said, "I must insist."

My dad flew the short distance to join us. "I'll tell the other fairies what we learned while you're with the elves, Blair. I'm sure it won't take long."

"No." I hesitated. "Bramble, how long has it been since we left?"

"Three days."

Three days? Dad had mentioned that the fairy realm tended to mess with time, but three days was long enough for any number of things to have gone wrong in Fairy Falls. There was no ignoring a summons from the king of the elves, however, so I followed Bramble into the forest.

While I stayed in my fairy form, I still had to duck to enter the tunnel that led to their home and walk at an awkward crouch until I came to the clearing where the elf king sat on his tree-stump throne. Like the others, he was dressed in bark-coloured clothing, though he wore an approximation of a crown upon his head.

He also held a sharp stick in his hand. That was new.

"Your Majesty." I bowed lopsidedly for the second time that day. "You wanted to speak to me?"

"What news from the Eventide Court?" he asked without preamble.

"Erm." I wished I'd known he expected a report, though that wouldn't have made it any easier to break the bad news. "Lady Eventide expressed her concerns and wished us luck with the upcoming fight."

An intensely awkward pause followed.

"Is that all?" The king leaned forward from his seat, disapproval etched into his every feature. "Nothing more?"

"I hoped she'd offer some help, but she thinks we have the tools here to fight Clearwater ourselves," I mumbled. "He's not threatening her court, not directly, and she and the other fairies have no allegiance to the covens."

"Did you not tell her that Clearwater threatens far more than the covens?" he enquired.

"I tried." You'd think the elven king would be less intimidating after I'd faced the magic of the fairies and walked away intact, but any effects of that courage potion I'd drunk had thoroughly worn off by now. "But she thinks the human realm is... erm, she said it was poison to her and her people."

A murmur of discontent travelled among the elves.

"I see," said the elf king. "You truly managed to glean nothing else from the fairies?"

My face heated. "I did—I did possibly find out something useful from those hunters. The ones your people helped chase off."

"And what is that, Blair Wilkes?"

"I think... it sounded like the hunters aren't taking orders from Mrs Dailey." I thought back. "Well, aside from those three, but they're kind of useless. The rest of them seem to be with Clearwater."

A wave of sharp mutters broke out at his name, and the elf king's eyes narrowed. "The witch has never held sway over the hunters."

"No, but I thought she was tight with Clearwater," I said, with the distinct impression that I was making a complete mess of this. "If they aren't working together, might it be easier to take them on?"

That might have been hoping for too much, but if the two

weren't as close as I'd thought they were, surely, it ought to count for something.

"They might," he said, "or not. I expected more from you, Blair."

"I did my best." Shame heated my face. "I wasn't sure I was even going to get out of there alive. Besides, what was I supposed to do, order them to fight for humans against their own kind?"

The elves themselves had only come around to the idea of standing alongside the other people of Fairy Falls in the fight against Clearwater fairly recently, and it'd taken no small amount of persuasion. I didn't quite dare mention that aloud, but after a short pause, the elves' king said, "Pity they could not be persuaded. She was quite correct that this realm is poison to their kind. Or parts of it are."

"In what way?" I racked my thoughts. "I know fairies aren't fans of some human inventions."

One of the first facts I'd learned about fairies nudged its way back into my mind. Wasn't iron deadly poison to them? I knew it didn't affect me as badly, but I'd had an infamous sneezing fit while polishing cutlery at one of many failed jobs. To fairies who weren't half human, though… okay, maybe they did have reason to be wary of a world where modern technology had even infiltrated paranormal communities.

"I expect Lady Eventide was wary of what might happen to her people if she brought them to war here," he said. "However, they might yet change their minds."

"I hope so. My dad will be able to contact them again if he needs to." I fidgeted, hoping for a dismissal but not willing to offend him by asking.

"Go in peace, Blair Wilkes." He bade me farewell.

I left the clearing with a mixture of guilt and relief. He'd given me one thing to think about, though. Fairies were weakened by iron. Would defeating Clearwater be as simple as stabbing him with a sword? I doubted it. I didn't know anyone who *had* a sword, for one thing, and he'd no doubt formulated plans to compensate for any weaknesses he might possess.

Still, between that and the revelation that all might not be well between Mrs Dailey and Rowe Clearwater, I'd take it.

5

As I left the forest, it occurred to me that I hadn't the faintest idea what time it was. Daytime, evidenced by the sun streaming downward, which meant most people would be at work. Including Nathan and perhaps Alissa too. Since I'd left my phone behind—and I was glad of it now, considering my dives into the lake—I went back home first.

Alissa wasn't in the flat. Neither was Sky, though Roald lay sleeping on the sofa as I entered the living room. I changed out of my wrinkled clothes and grabbed my phone, finding it cluttered with several days' worth of messages. The most recent was from Nathan, telling me he was out on patrol. I sent him a quick reply, saying I'd returned from the fairy realm in one piece. He must have been near the northern border, or else I'd have run into him on the way back.

I finished skimming through the messages and found no others from today, but when I ventured into the kitchen, I found a note from Alissa pinned to the fridge, saying she was at work. After a brief mental debate, I opted to check in on her first. The hospital was closer than wherever Nathan was patrolling, and besides, if I had to admit it, I wasn't yet ready to break the bad news to Madame Grey—not to mention Rebecca. Alissa was far better than I was at figuring out how to handle her grandmother, and with the way I'd screwed things up with the elves' king, I was in dire need of her expertise.

I entered the hospital, a squat building on the high street, and found the waiting room empty. There was just one exception: an elderly witch wearing a purple wig who stood in a corner with a dreamy look on her face.

"Did you have a nice trip, Briar?" asked old Ava.

"Erm…" Did she know where I'd been? As a Seer, quite possibly yes. "Are you supposed to be out here?"

"No," answered Alissa, who came running into view from the corridor. "I turned my back for one minute, and she sneaked out."

"I knew Briar was coming, you know," Ava announced.

"Of course you did." Alissa ran to me and hugged me. "You're back. Thank goodness for that."

"Sorry it's been so long." I hugged her back. "It's only been a few hours for me, not days."

Ava laughed. "Those fairies are tricky, aren't they?"

"You might say that." I let go of Alissa, eyeing the elderly witch. "I don't suppose you have any ideas about how to defeat an immortal?"

"The winged one?" Ava extracted her wand from her hair. "Try this."

"I can't take your wand." Not least because the nurses had replaced it with a fake one after too many accidents, though old Ava didn't seem to have noticed. "I appreciate the help, though."

"Come on, Ava," said Alissa. "Let's go back to your room."

Ava complied cheerfully enough for me to wonder if she'd been waiting to see if I'd returned safely too.

Alissa steered her down the corridor that led to her room and passed her over to another nurse before returning to my side. "So," she said, "how'd it go with the fairies?"

"Well, I'm alive."

"I noticed," she said wryly, though some concern flickered into her eyes. "It didn't go well, then?"

I shook my head. "I mean, it could have gone worse, but the fairies didn't think our issues were urgent enough that they felt the need to volunteer to help us out."

"Seriously?" she said. "Being on the brink of being invaded by an army of fairies and hunters led by an evil immortal wielding a sceptre isn't urgent?"

"Not according to them," I said. "Unless Clearwater shows up on their doorstep, Fairy Falls is too small an issue for them."

"Well, that sucks." She pursed her lips. "Have you told my grandmother yet?"

"No. I just got back." In my pocket, my phone buzzed. "I was trying to figure out how to break the news. I already had to tell the elf king."

"They don't give you a break, do they?" When my phone kept buzzing, she added, "I think you'd better answer that."

"Ah." I pulled out my phone. "It's Nathan. I'll see you later?"

"Sure thing," she said. "I'll let you know when my shift finishes. If my grandmother hasn't monopolised your attention."

"Of course." I had an inkling everyone would want a piece of me today, but I could at least check in with Nathan first. Answering the phone call, I walked out of the reception and into the street. "Hey, Nathan."

"Blair," he said. "I'm glad you're back."

"Me too," I said. "Are you still at the border? I can come and meet you when you're done with work unless Steve is generous and lets you go early."

"Actually, I need your help with something."

"Oh?" I heard several voices behind his, talking in the background. "What is it?"

"Is that Blair?" The voice, though quiet, was recognisable as Nathan's father's. And the other... was that his elder brother?

I stopped in my tracks. "Is your family there?"

"Yes," he replied. "They can't get in."

Given his calm tone, they weren't here to attack us on behalf of Clearwater, but that didn't mean he wasn't involved. "They want to talk to me?"

"Yeah," he said. "I'm sorry. I know you only just got home."

"It's no problem. I'll be right there."

Had his family shown up to convince us to surrender? Surely not. His dad, at least, was wise to the former Inquisitor's trickery. Mr Harker had helped me reveal Clearwater's real identity himself, in fact, but I had a hard time believing the others had shown up to pay us a friendly visit.

I didn't get my wings out, instead engaging my Seven Millimetre Boots to fly to meet them. I was acutely aware that I needed to report to Madame Grey sooner rather than later, but she wouldn't want me to let Nathan's request go ignored, either.

I flew northward, alongside the university campus on my left, which was circled by a high fence that came to an end at the northern border. On my right-hand side was the part of the forest in which the werewolves lived, and at the top of the slope, I spied Nathan. Opposite him stood his father and eldest brother, on the other side of the barrier that encased the town like a dome. They did not look pleased.

"Mr Harker." I landed at Nathan's side, facing his dad across the barrier. "Why are you here?"

The elder Mr Harker watched me with his usual expression of mild disdain, as if he couldn't fathom why his son had picked *me* as his partner. "Blair Wilkes. I thought you were absent on an errand for the witches."

I blinked and then smoothed out my expression. "That's right."

They didn't know I'd been to the fairies' realm. Nathan had promised to tell nobody outside of Fairy Falls, and his family members were no exception. I could only imagine what they might do with that information.

"Why exactly did you bring her here, Nathan?" Jay swivelled to face his younger brother. "To convince us to abandon our posts?"

I cleared my throat. "Why are *you* here?"

"We're here because Nathan has abandoned his duty," said Jay. "Erin too."

"What, by leaving the hunters?" I asked blankly. "Didn't Nathan leave years ago?"

"Circumstances change," said Jay. "Since the other people in Fairy Falls have thrown their lot in with a group of misfits and traitors, I would have expected him to have second thoughts about his choices."

"What?" Disbelief and shock rose inside me in equal measures. "Who called us misfits and traitors? Was it the former Inquisitor, by any chance?"

"The *reinstated* Inquisitor made a statement to the hunters, yes," said Jay. "Explaining that the witches betrayed us, and so did the entirety of Fairy Falls."

I glanced sideways at Nathan, unable to believe this drivel. "Did you all get collective amnesia about *why* the Inquisitor was driven away? He's a fairy who's been blackmailing and manipulating his way to power for literal centuries. I can't believe you fell for the same tricks twice."

"Precisely," Nathan said. "He used glamour to trick anyone who sees him into viewing him as human, no doubt, but you can't have forgotten the past so easily."

"*She* can use glamour." Jay indicated me. "I've seen her use it. I've never seen the Inquisitor do anything of the sort."

"You weren't there, but there were dozens of witnesses. Including Nathan himself." I looked pleadingly at Mr Harker. "Don't you remember when you gave me photographic evidence of the Inquisitor's real identity? The photo, showing he hadn't aged in years?"

"Yes." He eyed his eldest son. "Unfortunately, the photo was lost."

"Does he not believe you?" I frowned at Jay.

His jaw clenched.

"Don't you believe your own father or brother?" I asked him.

"I believe he was misled," said Jay. "No doubt through some trickery of yours."

"You're the one who was tricked." What had I done with that photo? Conor might still have it, or the witches, but it wouldn't matter even if I waved it in this guy's face. He'd claim it was a forgery or something, given that he'd already made up his mind.

Nathan shifted on his feet. "Dad, you need to stick to your guns. Stop letting Jay intimidate you."

"Intimidate me?" Mr Harker's face reddened. "Don't be absurd."

"He dragged you here, didn't he?" Nathan glanced towards me. "To convince me to abandon Blair."

Mr Harker's mouth pinched. "I simply believe you could do more good outside of Fairy Falls than inside, aiding the local hunters in the search for a better path and a new era of cooperation."

"Cooperation?" I echoed. "The Inquisitor—Rowe Clearwater, that's his real name—wants to wipe us off the map. There's no cooperating with someone like that."

"This town has been a problem area for a long while," said Jay. "I see nothing wrong with putting the hunters in charge."

"He's really done a number on you, hasn't he?" My hands fisted, anger burning away my disbelief. "You won't hear a word that contradicts what he told you."

Mr Harker cleared his throat. "I believe Jay was invited to speak to the Inquisitor along with the other leaders of the local hunter branches, as well as Eric and those who have been chosen for special missions."

All the local group leaders. That meant every group in the region had been blasted with Clearwater's glamour. No wonder they wouldn't hear a word against him.

"That's right," Jay said. "He made it clear who the real traitors are: you, the other fairies in this town, and that Madame Grey."

"And Sleepy, Dopey, Grumpy, and Mrs Dailey are all upstanding citizens, are they?" I couldn't help asking.

"Who?" Jay's brow furrowed in confusion.

"Three lowlifes and one of the prisoners your new leader set free from the LPFP." I tensed when Nathan caught my arm, realising that in my anger, I'd almost crossed the border of Fairy Falls and wound up outside. *Good catch.*

"What are you blathering about?" Jay shook his head. "Honestly. If you aren't going to come with me, Nathan, you and your sister are at as much risk as anyone else who stands in the Inquisitor's way. This is your last warning."

"Before what?" I asked. "What is he going to do, stand here and yell at us from the other side of the border until we surrender to get him to shut up?"

Jay's eyes narrowed. "This little spell of yours won't last forever. You'll see. It's a shame, Nathan. I thought you were better than this."

He turned his back and walked away, while Nathan stood rigid at my side. Mr Harker remained still for a moment, a hint of sadness in his expression, and then he left too.

"Clearwater's gone too far." By bewitching the head of every hunter branch in the area, he'd gained the ability to target us on several fronts at once. Nathan's father must have only avoided falling under the spell himself because he'd been retired, and even then, he hadn't been able to argue against his eldest son.

"Where *is* Erin?" I asked.

"She refused to come out and meet them." Nathan dragged his gaze from his departing family, regret etched into his face. "I'm sorry I dragged you into this."

"Don't worry about it." I pulled him into a hug, burying my head in his chest. "I'm glad you're okay. I swear it's only been a few hours since I left."

"You warned me the fairies would mess with time." He gave me a brief kiss. "How'd it go?"

I pulled a face. "I met my aunt. She refused to help us."

"Your aunt?" His brows shot up. "Your father's sister, I take it?"

"Yeah, turns out she's kind of the queen of the fairies now." I told him the rest as we walked downhill, in the direction of the witches' headquarters, finishing up with our surprise encounter with Sleepy, Dopey, and Grumpy at the border.

"Mrs Dailey and the former Inquisitor aren't working together?" he asked. "Interesting."

"I'm not sure they were ever friends," I said. "That's what I got from those three idiots, anyway. I assume Clearwater helped her escape jail in exchange for a favour, but they aren't working together, and she'll have her own plans."

"Ones that involve her daughter, I assume."

"Yep." I slowed down as we neared the witches' headquarters. "Speaking of whom, let's see if she's in here."

Rebecca might have been at school, but she'd been spending more and more time taking private lessons with Rita in recent days. No doubt that had only increased since my absence if Blythe had persisted in scaring her sister into thinking Fairy Falls would be attacked while I was gone.

"She is." Nathan indicated the downstairs window. "I should go and tell Steve about my family's visit."

"Bet he'll love that," I commented. "What're the odds that he'll find a way to pin the blame on me?"

"I won't mention you. Don't worry," he said. "I'll need to tell Erin too. See you later?"

"Of course." I hugged him goodbye and then entered the building.

When I walked into the classroom, Rebecca gasped and nearly dropped the sceptre in the middle of casting a spell. A jet of purple light shot out, burning a sizzling hole into the wall.

"Oops." I gave Rita an apologetic look. "Sorry. I should have knocked."

"Blair!" Rebecca ran to me and wrapped me in a hug while Rita waved her wand to fix the damage. "I'm glad you're all right. I thought something happened to you."

"Yeah. I'm fine. The fairy realm is in a different time zone." I didn't see Madame Grey this time, so I figured she must be upstairs. "Rita, is Madame Grey in her office?"

"She is, yes," the other witch replied. "She might be on the phone. A lot of people are trying to get hold of her."

"Including the regional witch council?" I stepped back

from Rebecca, my heart sinking at the memory. "Is—is the Seeing Stone still where it's supposed to be?"

"As far as we know," Rita said. "I do hope you've brought good news."

I swallowed my relief at seeing Rebecca evaporating swiftly. "No, not exactly. The fairies aren't going to help us."

"What?" Rebecca's face fell. "They aren't?"

I hadn't known she'd got her hopes up about them coming to our rescue or that the other witches had, either. "No, but I found out your mother isn't working with Clearwater. I found some of her spies at the border, who gave it away."

"Spies?" Panic flooded her expression. "Are they still there?"

"No—the elves chased them off," I said hastily. "Don't worry. I just thought it was interesting that Clearwater isn't helping her. They're more dangerous together than apart."

"But she wants me," Rebecca said. "Her people are looking for a way into the town so she can get at me, aren't they?"

Yes. Unfortunately. That wasn't news to either of us, though, and Clearwater stood a far greater chance of getting access to the town than Mrs Dailey's dimwitted hunter allies did.

"She won't get in," Rita told her. "You know that."

"Exactly." I wished I'd never mentioned them in front of her. "Those hunters wouldn't know a way into town if they fell into it."

She didn't smile, but her fearful expression dimmed a little. "Okay. I just… I hoped the fairies might help."

"They still might," I said. "Don't forget, my dad hadn't spoken to them in decades, and they'd never met me before."

Rita inclined her head. "I believe you should go and speak to Madame Grey, Blair."

"Yeah." Best to get it over with. "I'll be down in a minute."

Guilt twisted inside me as I left the room and went upstairs to Madame Grey, halting outside her polished wooden door. I knocked once.

She called, "Enter." Madame Grey showed no surprise when I walked into her office. "Blair. I thought I saw you outside earlier."

"Yeah. I only just got back." The words jammed in my throat as the sense of failure settled over me like a spectre. "I wish I had good news, but the fairies think we can handle everything on our own."

"I see." She studied me over the tops of her spectacles. "It's not surprising that they'd view the situation as of little concern to immortals such as themselves."

"Yeah." I bit my lower lip. "I'm sorry. I tried to convince them, but the leader of the Eventide Court has no love for the covens and can't fathom why any fairy would fight on behalf of humans."

"A not uncommon attitude, I gather," she said. "Now, why were you running through the high street earlier?"

"Erm…" Backtracking, I summed up our encounter with the hunters at the border and my talk with the elf king before explaining Nathan's family's unexpected visit.

She surveyed me for a long moment when I'd finished. "I suspected that Clearwater would make use of Nathan's family to strengthen his forces against us. I'm glad he didn't give in."

"Not just him," I said. "He's glamoured every single leader of each group of hunters in the region into obeying his commands and refusing to hear a word against him."

"Again, not unexpected." She drummed her fingers on the desk. "I *am* curious as to Mrs Dailey's involvement, however."

"I'd hoped they'd parted ways," I admitted. "Might be too much to hope for, but Clearwater has clearly commandeered the best hunters for himself and left her with the dregs."

"Yes, we'll look into that," she said. "I had one last question: where's that cat of yours?"

"Oh—I sent him to guard my foster parents," I said. "He offered to watch them while I was gone."

"Good thinking," she said. "However, I suspect that even a fairy cat would be unable to prevent Clearwater from targeting them."

"You think he'll try?" My throat went dry, though I knew she was right. He'd targeted Nathan's family, after all, and him going after mine next was certainly not out of the realm of possibility. "What should I do?"

"It's up to you," she said, "but there's only one place that you can guarantee their safety."

"In Fairy Falls."

Was it safe for them, though? Clearwater wasn't able to get in, but their last experience with the magical world had ended in disaster. If I brought my foster parents into Fairy Falls, would they be able to handle it this time?

I didn't know. But if Madame Grey believed they might be targeted, I might have no choice but to find out.

6

That night, I slept long and deeply, and my eyes cracked open to the slightly alarming sight of Sky the cat looming over Nathan and me. "Miaow."

"Sky!" I jerked upright, unintentionally jostling Nathan in the process. "Wait, where are my foster parents?"

"Miaow."

I didn't know what that meant, but I assumed from the fact that he wasn't panicking and herding me out of bed that they were safe.

Nathan looked blearily up at me. "Blair, what's your cat doing here?"

"I was wondering the same." I shuffled aside as Sky wedged himself into the bed between us. "I assume he traded places with someone else to watch my foster parents. That or he thinks they aren't likely to be attacked before..."

"Before what?" Nathan laced his fingers with mine over Sky's furry back. "What did you decide?"

I squeezed his hand. "I think it's safer for them to be here than outside, though 'safe' might be an overstatement."

For normals, the magical world was the exact opposite of

safe, but Fairy Falls was the only place close enough for me to ensure that Clearwater never got near them. Yet the question remained: how was I supposed to prevent them from a repeat of the first time they'd seen the magical world, when they'd been enchanted by a fairy and nearly lost their minds? When they'd seen my real face and screamed in terror?

"It won't be like the last time, Blair," said Nathan, sensing my disquiet. "It'll be within our control."

"How?" I asked. "How do I stop them from seeing anything weird? Knowing my luck, we'll have people duelling in the streets and werewolves getting into fights on every corner. Not to mention Clearwater might be waiting for the chance to strike while I'm outside of Fairy Falls."

"That's a risk," he acknowledged, "but if we do it right, we can get them to safety without anything going sideways. I'll get the security team to help too."

"I'll have to meet them in Sloan," I said, referring to the nearest normal town within walking distance of Fairy Falls. "The only way here is on foot, and it goes straight past the place where…"

Where they'd been put under a fairy's spell.

Nathan squeezed my hand again. "It'll be fine. I'll bring a team to meet you outside Sloan."

I raised a brow at him. "You don't think they'll get suspicious if I bring them to town with a full-on security escort?"

"From a distance. Your parents won't ask questions if I come with you, will they?"

I groaned and buried my head in the pillow. "This is too much. I was planning to tell them about the paranormal world soon, but not like this."

"I get it," Nathan said softly. "You wanted to be careful, and who wouldn't? But while they're here, there'll be more opportunities to bring it up naturally rather than hitting them on the head with it."

"Assuming the evil immortal fairy who wants to kill us all isn't waiting to ambush us outside."

"Miaow," said Sky, which probably meant I was being ridiculous.

"Yes, I know." I lifted my head and gave him a stroke. "I need to get it over with before Clearwater *does* show up. He didn't seem to notice my dad and I were gone."

"Exactly," Nathan said encouragingly. "He's got his own plans, and he knows he can't get into the town. He won't want to waste his time by hanging around outside."

"I hope you're right." I pushed upright reluctantly. I'd hoped to spend the morning snuggling with him, making the most of our time together before the next disaster. Nathan and I had had precious little time to ourselves lately. "I'll see what Madame Grey says. I didn't have much time to talk to her yesterday, though she's the one who suggested bringing them to town in the first place."

"I imagine she'll understand," he said. "The real person we need to convince is Steve."

"What?" I blinked up at him. "Why… oh no."

"He's the one who has the final say over the security team's actions," he added. "If I want to come with you, we'll need his permission."

"Seriously?"

"Miaow," said Sky, arching upright.

"What's that mean?" I swivelled towards Nathan. "I can take Sky with me. They won't question if my cat comes to meet them. Much."

"Have you told them yet?"

"I may have dropped a hint or two." That was a good point. "I'll call them."

"Really, Blair." He shook his head, a smile curling his mouth. "Most people would call their parents *before* they start making plans to bring them into the magical world."

"I have no idea what to tell them." That wasn't strictly true, but what I didn't know was how much to reveal and how to keep from letting my panic over the potential danger make them suspicious. "I guess it's better than going to ask Steve for permission to borrow his security team."

"Exactly." He planted a kiss on my forehead. "Leave that part to me."

———

Steve the gargoyle looked askance at me. "Absolutely not."

"You don't own Nathan," I pointed out. "He can do whatever he likes when he's not on duty."

"That doesn't mean you can borrow the rest of the team for your trivial concerns." He glowered down at Nathan and me as we faced him across the police station lobby. "If you want your parents to come to Fairy Falls, you should have picked another time."

"It's not trivial," I objected. "My foster parents are likely to be targeted by the former Inquisitor, and they're normals. They have no defence against him. The only way to stop him from being able to reach them is to bring them here."

My parents had been delighted when I'd called them with the news that I was ready for them to visit me, and they hadn't even taken much persuasion to come here within a few short hours. But Nathan had not had nearly as much luck convincing the grumpy gargoyle police chief that loaning his security team to a couple of normals was the best use of their time.

Hence why I'd reluctantly come here to talk to Steve myself. Given my failures with the fairies, I might have been hoping for too much.

"And what of all the other people who would be grateful

to be offered shelter here?" he enquired. "Should we open our doors to everyone threatened by the fake Inquisitor?"

"You know that's not what I'm saying," I said, irritated. "He wants me specifically, and he'll target anyone vaguely connected to me in order to get to me. Didn't Nathan tell you about his family?"

I knew he had, as we'd discussed the subject the night before, but Steve was unimpressed. "You didn't ask me to go to *their* rescue, I notice."

"My siblings can take care of themselves," Nathan said evenly. "Blair's foster parents are entirely unaware of the magical world."

Steve glowered at me, looking remarkably statuelike even in his human form. "You think this is the ideal moment to give them an introduction, do you?"

My hands curled into fists, but I refused to let him intimidate me. "No, but I don't want the former Inquisitor to brainwash them, either. And you know he'd try. He did the same to the hunters."

"He did." Steve swivelled to Nathan. "I notice your security team didn't fall over themselves to volunteer to get back their own missing colleagues."

I blinked in confusion. "Missing colleagues?"

"The gargoyles," Nathan said. "The ones who vanished during the attack."

My heart sank. I'd forgotten that Clearwater had snatched up some of Steve's fellow gargoyles as allies—or I assumed that was where they'd ended up, since none of us had seen them since the battle a few weeks ago.

"That's right." Steve sneered at me. "Forgotten about anyone outside of your little bubble, haven't you, Blair Wilkes?"

That was unfair. "I'm doing my best here, but I can't be in ten places at once. When we beat Clearwater, everyone will be set free, but I can't fight him if I let him take the most vulnerable people in my life and use them as hostages."

"Exactly," Nathan said. "If you have an issue with me taking a patrol, I'll ask for volunteers. I just thought you might like to help us choose the team. You can spare some people, can't you?"

"I beg to differ." The gargoyle narrowed his eyes at me. "If the worst happens and the enemy is waiting for this very opportunity, would you want it on your conscience, Blair?"

My mouth parted. I had no answer for that, but I'd wondered if Clearwater might strike while I was in the fairy realm, too, and he hadn't. At this point, every movement we made carried a risk.

"If he is, it's me he wants." I lifted my chin. "Then I'll be out of your hair."

"That'll be the day." He turned his back and walked away before firing words at Nathan over his shoulder. "Do as you like, but don't expect my gargoyles to help you."

"Someone's in a mood," I muttered to Nathan as we walked out of the police station. "Will you be able to find enough volunteers, do you think?"

"Of course," he said. "The team's getting a little stir-crazy from walking in circles around the border day in and day out. A trip to Sloan will do them good."

I just hoped I could say the same for my foster parents —and me.

———

"I didn't know you were bringing your cat, Blair," said Mrs Wilkes.

Sky meowed in reply and rubbed against her leg, drawing some attention from passersby. That was my fault for picking the shopping centre as our meeting spot, but it had been the easiest location for all of us to find, and I didn't *think* Clearwater would attack us in full view of a bustling town centre full of normals. I hoped.

"You know what he's like." I crouched and scratched Sky behind the ears. "Won't let me go anywhere alone."

"Miaow."

"Nathan is going to meet us just outside of Sloan." I straightened upright, beckoning Sky to walk alongside me. "Then we'll walk to Fairy Falls together."

"That's wonderful," said Mrs Wilkes. "I'm glad you're finally able to let us come over. You had some trouble with work, did you?"

"Well, I had another guest staying until recently." Not an invited one. I still didn't know where Aveline was or what she was doing, but I was fervently glad she wasn't around to witness my parents' arrival in town. "But she's gone now. Shall we go?"

Only I could see the other fairy cats slinking out of sight down alleyways and streets, watching out for trouble. I'd drawn the line at bringing the rest of the security team with me, but fairy cats were experts at sneaking around without drawing attention.

Unlike me. I'd flown here using my Seven Millimetre Boots and now had to remind myself not to switch them on by accident out of nervousness. It'd be a fine thing to go to these extreme lengths to stop my foster parents from finding out about the magical world only to start flying in front of them in public, but it was hard to hide my nerves when there was so much at stake.

Nathan met us as planned, and we began to walk through the countryside from Sloan to Fairy Falls. The open space made me acutely conscious of how anyone might swoop down from the sky and attack us, though the only glamour I saw was the fairy cats hiding themselves from sight so Mr and Mrs Wilkes wouldn't wonder why we were surrounded by a troupe of felines.

Nathan's team was somewhere nearby, too, but I'd asked him to tell them to stay out of sight. I'd also asked them to watch the part of the border where I'd run into those hunters yesterday, but the most nervous-making part was when we walked past the tree where my foster parents had fallen under a fairy's spell not six months ago.

They both stopped to stare at the tree as if they recognised the place, and it was all I could do not to grab their arms and haul them away.

"Come on," I said, my voice trembling a little. "We're nearly at the lake."

I kept one eye on the glittering expanse of blue, but my foster parents wouldn't be able to see it until we got to the other side of the magical wards surrounding the village. I'd learned that the hard way when I'd first moved here and had been baffled when a lake—not to mention an entire village— had popped up out of nowhere.

"This is where we met," Nathan said as we descended the hillside. "Blair and I met just over there."

As predicted, my foster parents began bombarding him with questions. I'd encouraged him to distract their attention while we walked through the magical wards. Two layers covered the town—the ones that had originally been here to hide the town from ordinary eyes and the most recent protective spell Rebecca had cast to stop anyone who meant us harm from entering. Mr and Mrs Wilkes grew more visibly confused as we got closer without any signs of the town appearing.

My misgivings grew too. I *hoped* this wouldn't backfire. They'd been here before, but they wouldn't remember the experience that well. They'd been under a spell at the time, and I almost wished I'd put one on them again. Pushing aside my doubts, I walked through the border with Nathan at my side—and my foster parents stopped dead in their tracks as if they'd walked into a solid wall.

Nathan and I had entered Fairy Falls, but Mr and Mrs Wilkes were stuck on the other side of Rebecca's security spell.

"What's going on?" I looked to Nathan, alarmed. Oh no.

"I don't know. It's never done that before."

Does the barrier think they mean harm? Ack. I should have asked Rebecca to help. Not that Blythe would have let her take the risk of undoing the barrier spell and leaving the town open to attack, but why had the spell locked out a pair of harmless normals?

"Need help?" One of Nathan's burly security guards walked over to us. "Is the barrier not letting you in?"

"Barrier?" Mrs Wilkes peered at the air. "I don't see anything."

"There's an, erm, forcefield," I invented. "It's so transparent that it looks invisible."

"That's very impressive," said Mr Wilkes. "Technology, eh? It's going to outsmart us if we're not careful."

"No danger of that," I said, trying to keep their attention on my face while Nathan and the guard conversed in low voices. "Remember that time I worked in an office and accidentally infected every computer in there with a virus?"

Mrs Wilkes laughed. "Yes, I remember that, Blair. You always did have a knack for trouble."

"That's me."

Out of the corner of my eye, I saw a flickering light spread over the barrier, and then my foster parents stumbled forward.

"Oh—wow!" Mr Wilkes goggled at the lake, seeing it for the first time. "Where'd that come from? Were those houses here before?"

"It's erm, tinted," I invented. "The forcefield. Anyway, we're here. See?"

To my relief, Mr and Mrs Wilkes gawped and exclaimed over the prettiness of the village and had taken off down the cobbled street before I could even thank the security guard who'd helped us out. I'd left Nathan behind, too, but I didn't dare let them wander out of my sight. It wasn't as if I could have warned every person in town to avoid casting spells or doing anything weird, after all.

"I can't wait to show you my house," I said, wishing there was a way to teleport them straight there before they ran into trouble. "Come with me."

I took them through the back streets to avoid passing close to the shops that sold wands and enchanted items. Luckily, they were as enraptured by the Victorian-style house as I'd hoped, forgetting the rest of the town entirely.

"This is all yours?" asked Mrs Wilkes, gesturing at the house. "It's massive!"

"No, only one of the downstairs flats, which I share with my friend Alissa," I clarified. "But it's enough for me."

"Is Alissa here now?" asked Mr Wilkes.

"No, she's at work, but she'll be back soon. She works at a hospital."

I ushered them into the flat and set about making them tea and fetching biscuits—anything to distract them and keep them indoors. Nathan still wasn't back, but he'd likely stopped to talk to the security guards who'd helped escort us to Fairy Falls from a distance. I messaged him, asking him to thank them on my behalf, and then joined my foster parents in the living room. When I had them sitting down with teacups in their hands, I might have relaxed… if not for the werewolf standing on my lawn.

On the other side of the window stood a blond man with shaggy hair who definitely wasn't an invited guest. *Oh, hell.*

Wait, where was Sky? I never really knew how my familiar would react to guests, even ones he knew well, but I could have used his help to get rid of this guy.

"Who's that, Blair?"

My heart sank. "I'll be right back."

I bolted for the door and darted outside to waylay the man. He was in human form, for a mercy, but it would have been just my luck for a random werewolf to shift on my lawn and expose my parents to the paranormal world in the most dramatic way possible.

"Excuse me," I said. "Not to be rude, but why are you here? This is my house."

"You're Blair Wilkes."

"I'm sorry, who are you?" He looked familiar, but I couldn't figure out where I'd seen him before.

The man looked a little put out. "Don't you remember me?"

"No." Wait. "Are you that guy who pretended to be a wizard?"

The werewolf flushed bright red. "I don't do that anymore."

"So I see."

Vaughn Llewellyn. That was his name. He'd been disguising himself as a wizard until my paranormal-sensing power had unintentionally unmasked him, and last I'd heard, he'd reluctantly gone to live with the pack. That had been more than a year ago, though. Why was he here?

"Anyway, I came here to give you a message from the chief," he mumbled.

"What does he want?" I sounded more snappish than I'd intended, but his timing could hardly have been worse. "Sorry. I have visitors. It'll have to wait."

"He said he saw the Head Witch acting strangely."

My heart missed a beat. "Rebecca?"

"Yeah, the girl. She's up at the border."

"What's she doing up there?" Oh no. Had Mrs Dailey come after her daughter while we were all distracted? "I'll be right there in a minute."

I darted back into the flat, nearly tripping over Sky in the doorway. "There you are, Sky."

"Miaow!" He clawed me in the ankle for the indignity, and I hopped into the flat with the impression that the universe was not on my side today.

"Blair?" Mr Wilkes rose from the sofa. "Who's that man outside?"

Wonderful. "Sorry—I just have to run an errand." I rubbed my ankle. "Can you wait there? I won't be long."

"Oh, we can come with you!" said Mrs Wilkes. "We'd love to see more of the town."

"Later—it's a work thing," I invented. "You'd find it boring. Sky, can you—?"

"Miaow." He planted himself on the sofa, somehow managing to sprawl on both of them at the same time. *Thanks, Sky.*

"Five minutes!" I called over my shoulder as I pelted from the house.

Rebecca.

Mind whirling, I locked the front door and then cast a spell to stop it from being opened from the inside for good measure.

Vaughn watched in confusion. "Did you just lock your parents in your house?"

"Yes," I said shortly. "Where is Rebecca, do you know?"

"The north border near the forest."

"Cheers." I tapped on my boots and glided along the street while he ran to keep up with me. "I didn't know the chief was watching Rebecca."

"Why wouldn't he be?" he puffed. "The Head Witch is the only thing standing between us and that evil inspector."

"Inquisitor—false Inquisitor." He must have known the rest; everyone in town did. Even the people I'd all but forgotten about, like Dritch & Co's former clients.

"You still have those boots?" he asked as I veered up the high street, my feet hovering above the cobblestones. "The same ones Wilfred used to have?"

Guilt momentarily stalled me. "Are you still in contact?"

Wilfred had been framed for murder, the same crime which Vaughn had nearly been arrested for—except Wilfred had been mind-controlled into committing the deed himself. I hadn't thought to check up on him since.

"Yeah, he's doing okay," said Vaughn. "We're in touch."

"So he knows?" I guessed that it was hard to keep a secret that extreme from someone. Poor guy. "Where's he now?"

"He moved out of town," he said. "To set up a bakery elsewhere."

"Right. I forgot that was what he wanted to do." At least one person had escaped Clearwater's attention, but it was a reminder that the magical world stretched far beyond our borders, and more than our town was under threat. "I'm glad he's doing well. Where's—?"

I glided to a halt, seeing Rebecca's small figure ahead of me. She held her sceptre in her hand and was walking directly towards a woman on the other side of the town's boundary.

Mrs Dailey.

7

"Rebecca!" I called.

But she didn't answer me. She kept walking, as if in a trance, up to where her mother waited at the border.

I tapped on my Seven Millimetre Boots, pushed them to their limits, but it was too late. Mrs Dailey's arms folded around her daughter, drawing her into an embrace.

I skidded to a halt, heart sinking into my shoes, and fumbled to grab my wand. "What did you do to her?"

Mrs Dailey regarded me coldly over the crown of her daughter's head. "Nothing. She came to me of her own volition."

A growl cut through the end of her sentence, drawing my eyes to the forest. Several furred werewolves peered out of the bushes, attention fixed on Mrs Dailey—yet Rebecca didn't react. Her expression was blank, her gaze fixed on her feet.

"What did you do to her?" I repeated, pointing my wand at Mrs Dailey. "Let her go."

"I'm not controlling her," Mrs Dailey said. "See?"

"Someone is." I kept one eye on the werewolves, who inched closer to the border. Could they leap on Mrs Dailey before she fled? Quite possibly, yes.

Mrs Dailey must have known it, too, because she wasn't moving. Despite Rebecca being within her grasp, she remained rooted to the spot.

"Rebecca." I tried to look into her eyes, but her head remained bowed. "Come on. You can fight her off."

"She can't," said Mrs Dailey. "Her abilities are no match for mine. She's coming with me."

"Where, exactly?" I challenged. "Not the fairy realm, surely."

"Of course not," she said. "I'm the new leader of the Knot-grass Coven, and I inherited their entire domain."

"What?" I stared at her. "You took over from Arabella? What did her family have to say to that?"

"They were in no position to argue."

"Because you had her *murdered.*" My hands clenched at my sides. "Or Clearwater did. Where is he? Or did you come here alone?"

"A mother and daughter should be together."

"She already rejected you," I pointed out. "And you had to resort to putting her under a spell to make her walk back to you."

"You wouldn't understand," she said. "You never knew your mother."

"Because of *your* allies." Which she knew full well. She was trying to get under my skin—and besides, she was wrong. I did understand. I'd brought my foster parents here to keep them safe—from her.

She smiled. "Yes, I wonder how that will work out for you."

My heart jumped again. "You—stop reading my thoughts."

I should have been more careful. It wasn't impossible to guard my thoughts against her, but it'd been a long time since the two of us had faced one another in person, and I'd grown complacent.

I'd also forgotten that it wasn't the worst ability she had at her disposal.

Mrs Dailey smiled. "That's right. I don't want to render my daughter an empty shell, but perhaps starting over is the best option."

"You'd do that to your own child?" She'd threatened to wipe *my* memories once, and in her current state, Rebecca had no defence against her mother.

"If necessary." She looked directly at the werewolves gathering at the edge of the forest. "I wonder, is the chief of the werewolves willing to sacrifice the Head Witch's memories? I suspect the shifters won't mind much. They were never fond of the covens."

Alarm blared through me. I didn't know what choice the werewolves would make when it came down to it. They might be set against Mrs Dailey and the hunters, but they had no particular loyalty to the witches, either.

"Nobody wants you here," I said to her, pushing down my panic. "Including Rebecca. If you have to brainwash her to get what you want, you'll only end up disappointed when she rejects you again."

Anger flared in her eyes. "That won't happen. I'll make sure of it."

"Didn't work out so well for you the first time around, did it?" I reached for my wand, not daring to take my eyes off Rebecca. "Even Blythe rejected you. And it sounds like the Inquisitor doesn't want to be associated with you, either."

"You know nothing of this, you foolish child." She beckoned. "Come, Rebecca."

I snapped my fingers, wings unfurling behind my back. "You aren't going anywhere."

All I had at my disposal was the element of surprise and the knowledge that the instant I got Rebecca back on the other side of Fairy Falls's boundary, Mrs Dailey would no longer be able to lay a finger on her.

I snapped my fingers again and pictured the forest closing in around Mrs Dailey like the illusion my dad and I had encountered in Lady Eventide's castle. I'd never created an illusion on that scale, and even I took an instinctive step back when the trees *moved* the way I imagined them, their branches reaching out to grasp Mrs Dailey.

She merely wrinkled her nose, knowing they weren't real, but the lapse in her attention gave me the chance to fly over the border to Rebecca's side.

"Come on." I tugged on Rebecca's hand.

But she resisted—not actively, but her feet remained planted on the ground, and the added weight of the sceptre made it hard for me to make her budge.

"Rebecca, you'll be safe with me," I urged.

Mrs Dailey waved her hand at the illusory trees as if swatting a fly. "Enough trickery from you. Leave my daughter alone."

"You don't really want her, do you?" asked a voice from behind the illusion.

The voice startled me so much that half my illusion slipped, but it didn't matter. Even Mrs Dailey stared at the elderly figure who'd appeared in place of the trees, a smug smile on her face. *Aveline.*

"You," said Mrs Dailey. "The failed Head Witch."

Aveline laughed. "Failed? I've held down a job longer than you have. And I didn't need to enchant my relatives to do it."

"She's not wrong." I tugged on Rebecca's hand again, wishing Aveline would step in and help rather than taunting

Mrs Dailey from the side. "You're outnumbered, Mrs Dailey."

Rebecca's mother lunged for her daughter, but Aveline moved with surprising speed, pointing her wand at Rebecca's mother. A flash went off, but the spell veered sideways without making contact with its target. Mrs Dailey must have protected herself in some way, but she'd given me an opening.

I pulled on Rebecca's hands with all my strength until she stumbled closer to the town's boundary. The sceptre threatened to slide from her grip, forcing me to grasp the end to keep her from dropping it as I hurried her over the border. Violet light dazzled my vision, and I hastily let go in case the sceptre retaliated against me for putting my hands on it—but we'd made it back into Fairy Falls.

"She doesn't have to come with me herself if she gives me that sceptre," said Mrs Dailey. "Rebecca, I'll take it off your hands. Give it to me."

"No." I stepped in front of Rebecca as she made to cross the barrier and approach her mother again. "It's bad enough that your old ally has a sceptre of his own. I don't suppose you know how he managed to claim it, even though he isn't a witch."

Mrs Dailey gave a soft laugh. "You know little of the sceptres, Blair Wilkes. It'll be your undoing. Come, Rebecca."

A chorus of growls arose, and the werewolves emerged from the forest to form a barrier between Rebecca and her mother.

Mrs Dailey backed up, evidently assessing her options. Fury rippled through her expression, and then, with a wave of her wand, she vanished.

I exhaled a sigh of relief. "That was a close one. Why'd she come alone?"

She'd known Rebecca was going to be here—and under a

spell too—but her plan hadn't taken into account the werewolves. I doubted she'd expected them to jump to Rebecca's defence.

"Because she expected to win her daughter back," said Aveline. "Why did you let someone put a spell on her?"

"I didn't *let* anyone do anything." I peered at Rebecca's face, but her expression remained blank. "One of the werewolves warned me."

"They had more sense than you did, in that case." Aveline pointed her wand at Rebecca.

I tensed when a green light ignited and squeezed my eyes shut against the blazing glow.

Rebecca gasped at my side. "What... what happened?"

I jerked my eyes open and released her arm. "Are you okay?"

Rebecca staggered away, almost dropping the sceptre. "My mother... my mother was here."

"You were bewitched," said Aveline without any sympathy in her voice. "Someone forgot to keep an eye on you."

Blythe. Rebecca's sister would be furious when she found out, but what had driven her to look away from Rebecca in the first place?

"Not everyone." I approached the werewolves, who'd begun to slink away into the forest again. "Thank you for watching out for her."

The nearest wolf growled in what I could only assume was a reassuring manner. It didn't *sound* like it, but the implication was clear. The chief, whether he liked it or not, had taken it upon himself to help protect the Head Witch. Despite the previous enmity between him and the covens, he and his werewolves had saved her.

"Do you remember who bewitched you?" Aveline asked Rebecca.

The girl was still shaking uncontrollably. "No," she

mumbled. "I was… I was walking to the witches' headquarters for a lesson. With my sister."

"Blythe?" Was she still there? "I'll find her."

Please let her be okay. I didn't like Blythe, but if whoever had lured Rebecca out of town had wanted to get her out of the way, I hoped fervently that they hadn't done so in a permanent manner.

As we descended the hill alongside the forest, I snapped my fingers to return to my human form in case my foster parents had got curious enough to come looking for me. My cat would keep them distracted, I hoped, but I didn't dare check up on them until I was sure Blythe was in one piece. Not to mention everyone else at the witches' headquarters.

I used my Seven Millimetre Boots to fly ahead of Aveline and Rebecca, down the high street, until I came to a halt at a street corner. There, Blythe stood frozen in midmotion as if someone had created a realistic statue, and next to her was—

"Vincent." My heart jumped into my throat. "What—?"

"Your knack for trouble is impeccable, Blair," the smartly dressed vampire remarked. "Did you do this to her?"

"Of course not." I pulled out my wand. "What were you doing? Didn't you think of helping her?"

"I thought she was practising being a statue."

"Someone put a spell on her," I told him. "The same someone who tried to capture the Head Witch."

If it had been an ordinary freeze-frame spell, I should have been able to undo it myself, but my hand was shaking so much that my first attempt to wave my wand conjured up a wave of glitter instead.

"You're on form as ever, Blair," said Vincent, picking some of it out of his hair. "I shall see you later, I assume."

"Vincent!" *Damn that vampire.* Luckily, my second attempt at the spell succeeded, and Blythe came to herself.

Lowering her hands, she blinked slowly. "Blair? What are you doing here?"

"Someone put you under a spell. Did you see?"

"No. Wait. Where's my sister?"

"With Aveline." I pointed to the two of them as they approached us. "She was up at the border—"

"What?" Blythe took off like a rocket.

I scanned my surroundings for any sign of the attacker. I doubted they'd stuck around, especially if Vincent had been in the area, but where were they? And how had they got into town?

My phone pinged with a message. *Nathan.* Ack. I'd left him at the border with the guard who'd helped me bring my foster parents into town. But what if our arrival had enabled someone to get inside and bewitch Rebecca? I couldn't think of another way for them to have breached our security, and when I checked my phone, I found a message from Nathan telling me the security team had been delayed by an incident at the border.

An incident. Mrs Dailey had manufactured a diversion to take the security team out of the way, and if not for Aveline and the werewolves, she'd have got exactly what she wanted.

———

"You have a traitor among you" were the words with which Aveline greeted the council.

Madame Grey had called an impromptu meeting when we'd brought a shaken Rebecca back to the witches' headquarters, though Blythe had point-blank refused to let her sister be dragged into a meeting while she was still in shock. The pair of them had gone into one of the adjacent classrooms instead while the rest of us gathered in the council room.

"That's an overstatement," said Madame Grey. "The person responsible for bewitching Rebecca and her sister isn't present in this room."

"I'd know if they were," added Vincent, who hadn't been lying when he'd said he'd see me later. The vampire occupied one of the few chairs that wasn't taken by the witches who sat on the council alongside Madame Grey. Chief Donovan sat at the opposite end of the table, as far from the vampire as humanly possible.

And then there was my dad, too, representing the fairies, while Bramble sat in for the elves. I'd spent the past hour telling different versions of the same story to everyone who wanted to know after I'd dashed home to tell my foster parents that I'd been called into a last-minute work meeting. I'd been relieved to find they hadn't moved since I'd left. My cat could only lie on them and stop them from getting up for so long before they got suspicious, but they had accepted my excuse cheerfully enough.

Even then, I didn't like leaving them alone, knowing that someone within Fairy Falls itself had bewitched Rebecca—and that we didn't know their location. They might not have been in this room, but once they'd got behind the barrier around Fairy Falls, there was no shortage of possible hiding places.

"Where have you been, exactly?" Rita asked Aveline. "Leaving the town when you did was a risky venture."

"Oh, that awful woman and her hunter friends don't care about a former Head Witch like me," she said dismissively. "Neither does that fairy, Clearwater."

"Where *have* you been, though?" I asked. "Why did you come back now? You didn't know Rebecca would be targeted, did you?"

"Not at this precise moment, no," she said. "However, it was only a matter of time before her scheming mother made a move, and not everyone agrees with letting a child hold the title of Head Witch, do they?"

Whispers bounced up and down the table like a ping-pong ball, and I glared at Aveline. "Nobody here was responsible. If I had to guess, the intruder sneaked into town while someone else was causing a diversion at the southern border."

"Oh, yes, they would have," she said. "Unless the flaw lies with the security team. Aren't you involved in a romantic tryst with one of them, Blair? Or is that over?"

Leave it to Aveline to turn the tables by bringing up my love life in front of the entire council. "Nathan is dealing with the police. I haven't asked him if the security team saw anything strange near the border."

"Now, why was half the team not where they were supposed to be in the first place?" Aveline queried. "I wonder…"

I felt myself flush. She must have heard me mention I'd brought my foster parents to town, but she'd evidently decided I needed to repeat the story for the entire council to judge me on. Never mind that Nathan had gathered a team of people who *weren't* already patrolling to help me bring my foster parents into town.

"They were before someone distracted them," Madame Grey said evenly. "Someone working with Mrs Dailey, though I'm not convinced she doesn't retain connections with Rowe Clearwater despite their diverging goals."

"They aren't working together?" asked the werewolf chief sharply. "I thought Clearwater and the Dailey woman were allied from the start."

"They've worked together in the past," I said, "but Mrs Dailey's main target is Rebecca. Clearwater mostly wants me."

The werewolf scowled, no doubt irritated that the pack

had been dragged into this. He'd had to make some serious compromises in recent days, but I couldn't shield his hurt feelings when there was so much at stake.

"And our ability to protect ourselves is contingent upon Rebecca's safety," added Rita.

"Plainly, there was some neglect involved," said Aveline, who seemed determined to rile up everyone instead of making useful suggestions.

"I'm more interested to know why you waited until now to tell us that Mrs Dailey has taken over the Knotgrass Coven." I raised my voice, cutting through the murmurs that arose among the other witches at Aveline's words. "Or rather, waited for Mrs Dailey herself to tell us. You knew, right?"

This time, the mutters took on a different tone, aimed at Aveline herself, but she remained unmoved. "If you think a decrepit former Head Witch like me could have single-handedly defeated the magic of a powerful coven in the hands of an already powerful witch, you severely overestimate me, Blair, dearest."

I wasn't in the least bit fooled by her "woe is me" act, and neither was Madame Grey. "You might have warned us, like Blair said. And you still haven't answered the question as to where you've been all this time."

"I was finding the sceptre's creator, of course."

I had the distinct impression she'd been waiting to drop that information for maximum impact. Shocked whispers reverberated through the air, and even Madame Grey looked taken aback.

"I thought… I didn't know the person who created the sceptre was still alive," I said. "I thought they didn't make them anymore."

"Retired doesn't mean dead," said Aveline with a meaningful look around at the council members. "Despite what some of you might think."

"But I thought it had been hundreds of years," I amended. "That's a long time. Even for a witch. It *was* a witch, wasn't it? Or a coven?"

"Yes, and I know how to find their last living descendent," she said. "And I believe she might have a way for us to stop that nuisance of a fairy from using the sceptre he stole to destroy us all."

8

Aveline sat back smugly as exclamations of shock rang through the council meeting room. Rita was first to ask, "And how exactly do we find the descendant of the sceptre's creator? Have you met them?"

"No, of course I haven't," she replied. "They're well hidden, but their names show up in historical records."

"The Primrose Coven," Madame Grey said slowly. "I've read the name, but I've never heard of anyone making a claim to be a descendant."

"They wouldn't make it that easy, would they?" Aveline said. "Once I found the name, I knew I had to come here. I believe this town contains the resources necessary to track down the coven."

"So you *don't* know where they are." My shoulders slumped. "You only know that they exist. Possibly. That's way too vague for my liking."

"I agree with Blair," Madame Grey said to my surprise. "In any case, our priority should be finding whoever put a spell on the Head Witch before they try the same again. I intend to meet with the security team to determine precisely what happened today. Does anyone else have any questions to ask?"

Nobody did, for a wonder. The events had shaken everyone up, and while the question of how to find the coven that had created the sceptres would no doubt be the main subject of a future meeting, the final decision would be Rebecca's. When she'd recovered from the shock, that was.

At least we knew where to find Mrs Dailey herself if we wanted to, but that didn't change the fact that she was more powerful than I'd given her credit for, and she'd no doubt use the Knotgrass Coven's house's magic to her advantage against anyone who tried to find her.

As the meeting broke apart, Aveline made for the door first with a determined stride, as if she had somewhere to go. Like… oh, crap. My house.

"Erm, Aveline." I caught up with her in the lobby. "I already have my foster parents staying at my flat. I don't have space for anyone else. Sorry."

"Can't they stay in one of the other flats in the building?"

Well, technically, yes. "They're potential targets, too, until we catch Rebecca's attacker. I don't want to leave them out of my sight until they're safe."

She scoffed in response. "Perhaps I'll go, then. I wouldn't want to trespass upon Fairy Falls's hospitality."

Was she seriously threatening to leave town over her supposed right to take over my home? "Go right ahead and see if Mrs Dailey's forgotten that you stopped her from taking Rebecca. She might not be so willing to overlook you next time."

Aveline burst out laughing. "You've grown a spine, Blair. Good. You'll need it."

As she continued to walk, I fell into step with her. "Where are you going, then? Because I'm not joking. My parents are staying at my house, and they're normals. I'm trying to keep them from seeing any magic, and—"

Aveline gave another bark of laughter. "Good luck with *that*, Blair, dear."

"The Inquisitor wants them as his hostages to get me to surrender," I said heatedly. "He already has Nathan's family, and I'm his main target. I didn't have a choice."

"It sounds like your decision enabled the Head Witch's mother to strike at her while your backs were turned."

"You didn't have to tell the entire council," I hissed, conscious that we weren't out of hearing distance of the other council members yet. "Mrs Dailey would have kept trying to create a diversion until she got in no matter what. She clearly had this set up, especially if she's pulling strings with the Knotgrass Coven."

"Good."

"What do you mean, *good?*"

"If she has her attention on the other covens, it means she has no idea that we're searching for the coven that created the sceptre, of course."

"You haven't said *how* we're supposed to find them." I'd about had it with her nonsense and had had to resist the impulse to shut the door in her face when I left the witches' headquarters.

"Now, you're just being picky." Aveline stuck her walking stick in the doorway and joined me outside. "Where's she going, I wonder?"

I followed her gaze and saw Madame Grey walking in the opposite direction. To meet with Steve, I assumed. "To see if the police have caught the intruder yet. Feel free to come with us if you want some entertainment."

Hardly my preferred option, but it was better than Aveline going to my house and terrorising my foster parents.

I figured it'd serve her right if Steve and the gargoyles ran her out of town.

I made my way through the street to the police station, where Madame Grey had halted in the doorway. Inside, Nathan appeared to be arguing with Steve, who was in his gargoyle form. His huge wings dominated the lobby, making him look even more intimidating than usual, and if I'd had to guess, Steve was *not* pleased that someone had slipped past security. Uh-oh.

The doors slid open ahead of Madame Grey, and she strode into the lobby, while I trailed her. At my shoulder, Aveline snickered loudly enough that I wished I knew the spell the intruder had used to turn Blythe into a statue so I could use it on her.

"What exactly is going on in here?" Madame Grey enquired.

"I'm trying to get to the bottom of a security breach," Steve growled. "Someone created a diversion in the form of what appeared to be a flock of pigeons."

"Pigeons?" I asked. "That's what drew the entire security force to the southern border?"

"Giant ones," Steve said in tones that suggested this was no laughing matter whatsoever. "With claws."

"Still." I raised a brow at Nathan, spying several other people behind him, including Erin and Buck. They must have ducked out of sight to avoid being clipped in the face by one of Steve's massive wings. "It was Mrs Dailey's work."

Steve made an irritated noise. "If you hadn't monopolised my security team for your own trivial purposes, this wouldn't have happened."

"We're not *your* security team," Erin informed him. "In fact, most of us were off duty at the time. We volunteered to help Blair."

"Then one of you let an intruder in." Steve's wings

bumped against the ceiling as he swivelled towards me. "Unless Blair did that herself."

"Don't be absurd," said Madame Grey. "Blair brought her foster parents here under the assumption that they'd be safe."

"They couldn't get through the border at first," I recalled. "Then someone let them in."

"Evidently, someone else was waiting for the opportunity to strike," Steve added.

A soft laugh came from behind me—Aveline, of course—but I ignored her. If I'd had to guess, one of Mrs Dailey's allies had been lurking near the border, out of sight, waiting for an opportunity to sneak in. It made my blood run cold to imagine someone else being that close, though they hadn't been waiting to attack my foster parents after all. They'd been sneakier than that.

"There's a simple way to tell if the person responsible is in this room," Madame Grey said. "Blair, ask them if they saw anyone."

Right. My lie-sensing power would tell me if anyone here was being less than truthful, even unintentionally.

Steve's glower deepened.

But I spoke up, addressing everyone behind him. "Everyone tell me where you were at the time of Mrs Dailey's attack."

As they began to speak, I listened for anything that tripped up my lie-sensing power, but I had an inkling the intruder wouldn't have hidden in such an obvious place. No, they'd be elsewhere. And if Rebecca was the target, I knew they'd be biding their time until they could strike again.

———

The intruder must have known we were onto them. Despite the best efforts of the security team, not a single trace of whoever had attacked Rebecca materialised during their search of the town. I helped with part of the search but eventually went home out of guilt over leaving my foster parents alone.

Mercifully, Aveline hadn't invited herself to stay again. Probably because she'd taken it upon herself to hover outside the witches' headquarters, watching out for intruders like a hawk and shouting criticism at anyone else who came within sight of her. If anything, that should have been my cue to tell my foster parents about the magical world's existence, but I drew the line at letting Aveline dictate the terms.

Instead, I kept them occupied by digging out an old box of puzzles, while Sky kept showing up in random places and demanding pets. I was proud of myself for finding ways to keep them entertained without them realising I was on the lookout for a criminal, but by evening, I almost wished the intruder would show up on the doorstep just to get it over with.

I had to start somewhere, so that evening, I invited Mr and Mrs Wilkes to come with me to the pub. This was also my chance to give them a tour of the main high street, because most of the shops were closed, and it was harder to see the weird nature of the products on offer in the dark. I still had to drag them away from a broomstick display before they realised it was for flying and not for sweeping, but the sight of the Troll's Tavern pub soon made them forget everything else.

"Did that plate just fly?" asked Mr Wilkes as I steered them towards a table in the corner.

"No—it's magnetic," I invented. "This place is, erm, owned by magicians."

"Marvelous," said Mrs Wilkes, looking around at the oak tables and the array of paranormals sitting around us. "How quaint. Is that a wolf?"

"Puppy." I needed to distract them. "Ah, I have some bad news. I've been called into work tomorrow."

"Really?" Mrs Wilkes's face fell. "I thought you had the week off."

"Something came up." Guilt twinged inside me. "You know I work for a recruitment firm, and things are busy in summer. There's a bunch of university graduates who need our help."

Graduation wouldn't technically happen for another month, but I was prepared to invent a fictional university if necessary. Anything to stop them from realising that I would actually be spending tomorrow scouring the town for an intruder. If the trespasser didn't get caught tonight, I'd have no choice.

"Interesting," said Mr Wilkes. "Well, we can entertain ourselves, right?"

"Yes. I'll ask my dad too." He wouldn't mind giving them a tour of the forest, maybe the lake, though he'd have to be careful not to let them see any of the other fairies without their human glamour on. Mr and Mrs Wilkes had already met my dad, and I was sure they'd begun to suspect he wasn't *quite* normal, but that didn't mean they needed to dive into the deep end.

"He lives near the lake, you said?" Mrs Wilkes queried. "I'd like to have a closer look. I'm sure I saw someone swimming in there before."

"So did I," said Mr Wilkes. "And it *is* strange that we couldn't see the lake until we got close to it. I thought my eyes were playing tricks on me."

"Right." This ought to have been my cue to start telling them the truth, but the words tangled in my throat, and my heart raced like a jackhammer. Last time, it'd gone so badly wrong, and given the way today had gone already, I felt like I was sitting on the receiving end of a Lucky Latte's backlash.

"Yeah, when I first moved here, I thought the same. The bus driver couldn't even find Fairy Falls. I had to walk."

"Yes, it's an interesting name, isn't it?" Mrs Wilkes said. "Fairy Falls. I looked it up, you know, but I couldn't find anything on the internet."

"Ah." I should have guessed they'd get curious once the real name of my new home came out. "That's the reason for the name, but I didn't know that when I moved here. I didn't know a lot of things."

"Like what, Blair?" asked Mrs Wilkes. "What's wrong? You look pale."

I sucked in another shaky breath. "Some people here are… different. Most people, actually."

And with spectacular timing, three wine glasses appeared on the table. Mr and Mrs Wilkes exclaimed in shock, jumping to their feet, which drew the eyes of everyone in the vicinity.

"What was that?" Mr Wilkes asked, looking wildly around. "Where'd they come from?"

"That's a good question." I jumped upright myself when a flask appeared on the table to accompany the glasses, and out of the corner of my eye, I saw Alissa sidle out of the pub. The flask. The potion of courage. I wasn't entirely sure this was the scenario Lizzie had designed it for, but if I'd ever needed a shot of courage, it was now. Not just me, either. I wasn't the person who was about to have their entire world upended.

"What's this?" Mrs Wilkes picked up the flask.

"Mine. A coworker gave it to me." I reached out for the flask and tipped the contents into each of the glasses. "If you drink it, it'll help with what I'm about to say to you."

Mr and Mrs Wilkes's expressions remained confused, but they obeyed and sat down. I handed the glasses to each of them and then lifted my own, downing the sweet-tasting potion. My nerves stilled, and my heartbeat calmed. I *could* do this.

I looked at my foster parents. "So there are a few things I've been meaning to tell you."

———

That could have gone worse, I thought the next morning as I left my house. I'd let my parents sleep in late, trusting Sky to watch them when they eventually woke up. It'd been a late night, as I'd let them ask all the questions they wanted to while steering clear of the topic of *why* I'd picked this precise moment to bring them into Fairy Falls. I wouldn't have minded a lie-in myself, but we still had an intruder to find, and I was sure that a certain former Head Witch would be waiting to pay me back for not letting her stay at my home.

I entered the witches' headquarters and found Aveline sitting at the head of the table in the council meeting room as if she was Head Witch and not Rebecca. The Head Witch herself was there this time, though she and Blythe sat at the far end of the table and were engaged in a whispered conversation. Madame Grey also sat beside Aveline, and on her other side, inexplicably, was Veronica.

"Ah, Blair," my boss said to me. "Come on in. We were waiting for you."

"Okay." I stepped into the room warily. "Are you here to help find the intruder?"

"I heard that you were looking for the descendants of the Primrose Coven."

"Who?" I looked to Madame Grey, whose expression of mild annoyance suggested Aveline had been irritating her all morning. "Are they the coven who created the sceptres?"

"Yes," said Madame Grey. "Veronica believes she might be able to track them down."

"I thought you didn't know if they still existed," I said to my boss, wondering how she'd ended up being dragged into this. "You said they were likely to be long dead."

"Oh, the ones who actually *have* the gift are long gone, I expect," said Veronica. "But their descendants survive, and the former Head Witch reminded me that I have the means to find their location."

"You do?" I frowned at Aveline.

She chuckled. "That doesn't mean they'll work," she said. "The Primrose Coven won't *want* to be found, least of all by the sceptres' current wielders."

"Why?" I caught Rebecca's eye, seeing that she looked equally puzzled.

"Because they're trying to distance themselves from what their ancestors created, I assume," Blythe spoke up. "I would if I were them."

Given her mother, she'd know, I supposed. "We could use their help, though. Do they know that?"

"I doubt they care," said Aveline. "Hence why someone needs to persuade them."

That didn't work out so well with the fairies. Not that I needed to give her more ammunition to use against me by revealing my failed meeting with Lady Eventide.

"Not my sister," Blythe said. "This is ridiculous. Why are we wasting our time talking about this supposed coven when there's an intruder in town?"

"Because talking to someone who understands the sceptre might be our last chance to figure out how to beat Clearwater," Rebecca protested.

"You aren't leaving town even if we do find this missing coven," Blythe said flatly. "You know that's what our mother wants you to do."

"We need to know the actual location first." I turned back to Veronica. "Can you really find them?"

"I believe I can, yes."

She'd said as much before, reminding me that when she'd first recruited me to work for Dritch & Co, she'd picked me out as magical despite my otherwise mundane existence. Who knew, maybe her extensive network would be able to find a coven that had no intention of being found. But was that really our priority at the moment?

"Apply yourself to the task, Veronica," Madame Grey said. "Aveline, do you wish to help? Or would you rather assist us in finding the intruder?"

"I'm too old to run around chasing criminals."

As I began to reply, a roaring noise came from outside, loud enough that the entire room seemed to tremble. I thought it was a werewolf at first until I made out the word *MIAOW.*

"Sky?" I ran for the door, disbelief coursing through me. Hadn't he been with my foster parents? *What happened this time?*

I heard Rebecca calling my name as I fled the room, but I didn't dare turn back. The echoes of the roaring noise reverberated in the air while I ran out of the building and then picked up speed, pelting towards home.

On the lawn outside my house, Sky's monstrous form pinned down a terrified-looking woman with a giant paw. My paranormal-sensing power pegged her as a witch—right as I noticed my foster parents watching from the window.

I waved sheepishly at Mr and Mrs Wilkes. So much for giving them a break from the mayhem. They gaped at Sky as if he was a giant monster that had come to eat them, which was half true. The first half, that is.

Sky meowed again, more quietly this time.

I groaned. "Sky, who is this?"

"Call him off!" howled the witch. "Help!"

"Who are you?" The truth filtered in. "Are you the one who bewitched Rebecca? You're working with her mother?"

The witch nodded frantically. "Yes. She told me to bring the Head Witch to her. Let me go! I'll tell you everything!"

"Tell me why you're at my house." My eyes narrowed as my suspicions deepened. "You know my parents are in there, don't you?"

Sky growled, his claws at her throat, while the witch let out a faint whimper.

"Fine. You can talk to Madame Grey instead," I told her. "In fact, you can talk to Rebecca."

9

———

Sky herded the intruder towards the witches' headquarters while I briefly ducked into the house to check on my foster parents.

"Was that your cat, Blair?" asked Mrs Wilkes. "He was huge!"

"He's a fairy cat," I said, opting for honesty. "He's actually the size of a real cat, but he can pretend to be bigger to scare off intruders."

"Who was that?" Mr Wilkes pointed towards the window. "The woman outside?"

"An intruder." No point in pretending otherwise. "Really sorry, but I'll have to tell you the rest later. I need to make sure she doesn't get away."

I knew I was setting myself up for another interrogation, but it'd been just a matter of time before the truth of the situation in Fairy Falls came out. I wished we'd had more than a day, but that was what I got for bringing them to town in the middle of a crisis.

The sound of beating wings greeted me when I left the

house again, and when I caught up to Sky, a gargoyle came swooping down and landed in front of us. Steve bared his teeth at the witch, who swayed on her feet as if she might faint. "You caught the intruder, did you?"

"How did you know?" I supposed Sky's roar hadn't exactly been subtle, but I hadn't known Steve was paying attention. "We're taking her to Madame Grey."

"You certainly aren't," he said. "She broke the law in my town, and she'll face justice at my hands."

That figured. "That can wait until after we've found out how she got past the barrier spell."

"Hey!" Blythe came running into view from the witches' headquarters, evidently having heard the ruckus. "Who's that?"

"The witch who put a spell on your sister," I answered. "She was after my foster parents. My cat caught her and was bringing her to Madame Grey."

"Miaow," Sky growled.

The witch whimpered and shrank back.

Blythe stalked towards her. "I think my sister should be the one to interrogate her, don't you?"

"Precisely what I was thinking." I took a step back when Steve beat his wings, sending air gusting into our faces.

"I am the head of the police, and I have had enough of being undermined," he bellowed.

"You're a joke." Blythe reached for her wand, and just as I wondered if I was about to witness a fight between Blythe and Steve, Sky interrupted by emitting a rumbling growl like a lion about to pounce.

"That's enough!" I jabbed a finger towards the witches' headquarters. "Steve, if you want to sit in on the questioning, you can come along. It won't kill you to let Rebecca question the person who tried to bewitch her, will it?"

"And me," added Blythe.

"Why should I let *you* take over *my* job?" Steve wanted to know.

"I can read her mind, you blithering idiot," she told him. "I can get answers ten times as fast as you. For instance, did you know that she was going to bewitch Blair's parents into luring her out of town next?"

"Luring me out?" My attention snapped to the witch, forgetting Steve's ire. "Why me? I thought it was Rebecca she wanted."

"I'll find out." Blythe glowered at the witch.

Sky nudged his captive further towards the witches' headquarters.

"What are you plotting, I wonder?" Blythe mused.

"Tell me at once," Steve growled.

Blythe kept glaring at the witch as she walked, but then she came to a dead stop, narrowly avoiding a collision with the doors. "No, that can't be possible."

"What?" I pushed the door open, allowing Sky to nudge the cowering witch over the threshold.

Steve loomed behind me. "Yes, what?"

"What did you see in her head?" Possibilities rocketed around my mind, each more dire than the last. Behind the doors, I saw Madame Grey approaching us from across the lobby.

Blythe drew in a breath. "The Inquisitor has gone after the Seeing Stone... and the regional witch council."

My mouth fell open. "What?"

"Who is this?" Madame Grey came to a sharp halt in front of the witch, hardly seeming fazed by my cat's giant form shadowing the doorway. "The intruder?"

"Yes—and Blythe read her mind." I ignored Steve's grumbling behind me and walked to Blythe's side. "Clearwater's gone after the Seeing Stone."

Madame Grey took a step back. "Impossible. The council stored the Stone in a secure location."

"Ask her." Blythe pointed at the cowering witch. "She bewitched my sister, which means Rebecca should get to interrogate her, right?"

"She was going after my parents too." She had been following Mrs Dailey's orders, not Clearwater's—right? "To lure *me* outside the town, apparently."

"Looks like she wanted to use Blair as bait," Blythe put in. "As if bewitching a child isn't screwed up enough."

"She's the Head Witch!" the intruder burst out. "I didn't know she was really a kid."

"You still cursed her." Disgusted, I turned to Madame Grey. "Do you want us to help interrogate her? Or should someone go and check if what she said is true?"

"I'm the head of the police!" Steve objected. "She's supposed to be my responsibility."

"Then I suggest you take your duties seriously and go ensure nobody else has managed to slip through your security," Madame Grey said.

Steve flushed bright red, and Sky growled pointedly. I didn't really want to know who'd win in a standoff between the pair of them, but Steve must have figured he was outnumbered. He slunk outside.

I stepped up to Madame Grey. "Should I go and see if Clearwater has gone after the Seeing Stone? If he gets his hands on it…"

He could use it against any fairy and bring them under his control. Between that and the sceptre, I didn't know how we could possibly beat him if the intruder's claims turned out to be true.

"The Seeing Stone is in a secured house," she said. "I find it hard to believe he could have broken inside without word having reached me."

"He's capable of it, though, right?"

"Of course he is, but that doesn't mean this isn't a potential trap intended to lure us out of Fairy Falls." Madame Grey indicated one of the empty classrooms. "Take her in there, won't you, Sky?"

"Miaow," Sky growled, nudging the witch into the classroom.

Blythe followed.

I hung back. I wanted to hear what the witch had to say, but if she'd told the truth, if Clearwater already had his hands on the Seeing Stone, we needed a plan. Fast.

Rebecca came hurrying out of the council meeting room. "What's going on?"

"We caught the intruder," I told her. "Blythe is in there with her, and you can help question her if you want to."

She went pale then nodded. "Sure."

Madame Grey and I also joined Rebecca and her sister in the classroom, where the witch had sunk into a chair, Sky looming over her like a giant furry prison guard.

"Talk," Blythe commanded. "What were you going to do once you lured Blair out of Fairy Falls? If you lie, I can get the truth out of your thoughts one way or another."

"I was improvising," the witch gasped. "She—my boss told me not to come back to her without the Head Witch. When her plan failed, I didn't want to leave the town in case I couldn't get back in. There were too many people watching the Head Witch, and when I heard there were normals…"

"You thought they'd make good bait?" Anger sparked inside me. "Then what? Were you going to use *me* as bait for Rebecca? Did you expect to be able to single-handedly take down me and the Head Witch in one go?"

The witch cringed away from Sky's giant paw. "I didn't know you had a… what *is* this?"

"Miaow," growled Sky.

"A fairy cat," I answered. "Was that the extent of your plan?"

She nodded frantically. "Yes. Like I said, I was improvising."

"What about Clearwater?" I asked. "Is he working with Mrs Dailey or not?"

The witch lowered her gaze. "I haven't met him, but my boss… she knows what he's doing."

"Going after the Seeing Stone," Blythe cut in. "Right? That's his plan. Is he there right now?"

"I don't know," she whispered. "He's been trying to figure out how to get hold of it for weeks, she said, but it sounds like he might have found a way to…"

"To what?"

"To bribe someone into letting him in."

My heart plunged into my shoes. "One of the witches on the council?" One of Mrs Dailey's former allies, I was willing to bet.

"Or their confidants," added Blythe. "Hiding an object that powerful is hard to keep secret."

The witch bowed her head. "Yes. He might face opposition, but it sounds like he's determined to try. But if you need my help, I can—"

"Screw that," said Blythe. "You killed your chances of being an ally when you cursed my sister."

"We'll pick this up later." Madame Grey swept out of the room, beckoning to me to follow her.

"What should we do?" I whispered to her. "Do you want someone to check up on the Seeing Stone?"

"I can call the regional witch council myself," she said, "but if they don't answer the phone, the only way to see what's going on there is to travel to the location on foot. The entire area is warded against transportation spells."

"It is?" That might have explained why Clearwater had

taken so long to figure out how to get in. "I'd have to fly, you mean?"

"Yes, and there's a strong chance that Clearwater is counting on exactly that."

I bit my lip. "You know what'll happen if he gets hold of that Seeing Stone."

Her lips pressed together. "Yes, and if one of the council members has indeed showed him the way to its hiding place, he might face less opposition than I'd hoped. Five or six people know the location, and no doubt they'll be ready to fight him off, but if he brought his army…"

"He'll slaughter them." My blood iced over. "What can we do? Send an army of our own?"

"We'd never get there on time," she said. "Even if we did have an army to match his. Our one hope is that he has yet to get inside the safe house. If that's the case, we can move the Seeing Stone elsewhere."

"Is that doable?"

She inclined her head. "Yes, but it's risky. Most other people don't know the way to the witch council's safe house, either. I can name one person aside from myself currently present in Fairy Falls."

I frowned in confusion. "Who?"

"Someone who's stolen from them before."

The truth hit me like a slap to the face. "My dad."

"Yes." Concern glimmered in her eyes. "You and he might be able to reach the safe house before Clearwater does, but if he's already there, you have to flee."

"No way." I shook my head. "I can't. If he has that, he can control any fairy. Nobody will be safe."

"Please, Blair." Rebecca walked out of the classroom, gripping her sceptre hard. "You can't leave. Not when both Clearwater *and* my mother are out there."

"I—I can't let my dad go alone." Look what had happened

the last time he'd taken the Seeing Stone. If the witches saw him as an intruder, what then? "That's assuming he'll say yes, anyway. I have to ask him first."

Rebecca made a noise of protest, but I didn't dare stay a moment longer. I ran out of the witches' headquarters, and then I snapped my fingers to turn into fairy mode. Then I flew, scarcely stopping to breathe, until I reached the forest. From there, I sought out the route into the fairies' part of the forest and then flew straight up the path to my dad's house.

He opened the door the instant I knocked. "Blair?"

"Clearwater's going after the Seeing Stone."

Horror flickered in his eyes. "Now? Are you sure?"

I jerked my head in a nod. "Yeah. We caught the witch who cursed Rebecca, and Blythe read the truth from her mind. Clearwater is going to the safe house, and—and Madame Grey said you're the only person aside from herself who knows the way there."

"I do." He sucked in a breath. "I do, but last time…"

"You got arrested, I know," I said. "That's why I have to go with you. If you want to go, I mean. I know it must bring up bad memories."

"If Clearwater gets his hands on that stone, it'll be far worse for all of us." He stepped out of his house. "We can't delay."

"I know." Relief warred with dread and the heavy knowledge that in leaving the safety of Fairy Falls, we were playing into Clearwater's hands. Not to mention leaving Rebecca to the mercy of her evil mother. But the intruder was in custody, while Clearwater was still out there, potentially unopposed.

My dad and I followed the path back into Fairy Falls, and I filled him in on what we'd learned from the intruder while we made our way to the witches' headquarters.

Madame Grey waited outside, greeting my dad with a nod of confirmation. "Were you planning to fly straight to the safe house?"

"That's the plan," I said.

My dad nodded agreement.

"If he's there—Clearwater—what then? What should I do?"

"Come straight back here," she said. "Don't try to fight him."

Objections died on my tongue. I didn't think I could outrun Clearwater when it came down to it, but regardless, if we got the Seeing Stone before he did, it'd be worth the risk.

I made the mistake of looking past Madame Grey and into the building, where Rebecca watched with an expression of quiet devastation etched on her face. The image lingered in my mind as my dad and I took flight.

We rose into the sky, higher and higher, until the buildings of Fairy Falls became a patchwork below. I'd never flown this high up in my fairy form, and it was disconcerting to see the lake reduced to a puddle, the forest nothing more than a mass of green on its shores.

Even then, I sensed the moment we left the boundaries of Fairy Falls, a vibration in the air that left me feeling starkly exposed. We were out in the open, but I didn't see any other fairies in sight. Nor did I see Mrs Dailey or any of her spies. Yet.

Dad beckoned me to follow him, and we headed north, side by side, over fields and farms. We passed villages and towns and patches of forest, and the small blots of cloud floating below reminded me of how high up we were. I might have appreciated the view more if not for the urgency of our mission and the knowledge of what might await us on the other side.

In seemingly no time at all, my dad's flight path dipped, and he pointed a finger at what appeared to be a manor house that sat alone amid the fields. "The Seeing Stone is concealed inside, but the wards will stop us from approaching from above."

"Right."

As I swooped down over the forest that lay in front of the manor house, a sudden rush of déjà vu hit me. Hadn't I seen this very sight before? Myself flying alongside my father? Yes, in a vision shown by the Seeing Stone itself.

As the wind rushed into my back, I met my dad's panicked eyes.

"They're here, Blair. They're already here."

Winged figures flocked around us from above and all sides, preventing us from flying anywhere but downward, towards the manor house, where armed hunters waited.

Among them stood Clearwater, holding the Seeing Stone in his hands. The jet-black crystal ball gleamed under the sun, reflecting our descent.

Clearwater was in his fairy form, wings extended behind his back, green eyes aglow with malice. "I thought you'd try to stop me, Blair, but you're too late."

"Blair!" Dad shouted in warning.

The instant my feet touched the ground, hands grabbed my shoulders. The hunters seized both of us, wrenching us apart, and they pushed me in front of Clearwater.

His too-bright green eyes studied my face. "I hoped you'd show up, Blair, though I didn't think you'd be foolish enough to try to stop me."

"What did you do to the witch council?" I demanded.

He didn't need to answer. Anyone who'd been here had either been subdued or had surrendered—or worse. Except perhaps whoever had helped him get inside, but I could only see his allies around us. Fairies and hunters, all pointing their weapons at my dad and me.

With a faint smile, Clearwater held up the stone. "Now, you'll surrender to me," he said to my father.

Dad's body went slack in the arms of the two hunters who held him, his eyes blanking out.

"Stop!" I shouted as the hunters began to drag him away. "Don't—"

"There's one way to end this, Blair," said Clearwater. "Surrender yourself to me."

"No way." My hands clenched. "I won't allow it."

"Then your father's life is forfeit." He beckoned, and the hunters released their captive.

My dad remained standing without putting up a fight, without so much as looking at me. He was under total control of the Seeing Stone.

My heart twisted. I couldn't give him up. "What do you want from me? I'm at your mercy already."

"I want you to give yourself up, Blair," he said. "If you do, I'll leave your family alone."

"You want my dad too," I said. "And Rebecca. Her mother's your ally, isn't she? Or don't you care what she does?"

"Mrs Dailey is free to play whatever games she likes," said Clearwater. "I imagine that Madame Grey is far more likely to be able to outwit a single witch if she no longer has to worry about me, wouldn't you say?"

"She won't let you get away with this, either," I said desperately. "Besides, I found out you were here because I questioned one of Mrs Dailey's witches. Are you allies or not?"

"She paid more attention than I thought." A short pause. "I will tell Madame Grey the terms of your surrender myself. It should be relatively straightforward. She'll understand that it's better to leave me alone, and I'll extend the same courtesy in her direction."

"I can't trust you to keep your word." I was backed into a corner, though. Even if he did go on to threaten Fairy Falls, what hope did I have of besting him now? "Besides, why offer me the choice?"

"As opposed to using this?" He held up the Seeing Stone. "I can take away your will if you'd prefer to do it that way, but the outcome will be the same."

Light played across the stone's surface, showing me my own terrified reflection and Dad's beside me. He shook his head slightly, and the surface rippled. The black glass went momentarily blank, and then a different vision altogether pierced my eyes.

I faced Clearwater, who held the Seeing Stone in both hands. Power rippled from its surface, threatening to draw me in, but I shook it off, unravelling the threads of the glamour he wove.

He *couldn't* control me. That was why he needed me to surrender willingly.

I wrenched my gaze from the Seeing Stone and saw the grim anger in Clearwater's eyes, indicating that he knew full well what the stone had shown me.

"Last chance, Blair," he said. "Your father will pay the price if you don't surrender, which should make this an easy choice. Isn't that so?"

"Let him go," I said. "Let him return home to Fairy Falls. Leave his family alone too."

"Oh, I don't think so," he said. "I only promised to leave Fairy Falls alone, not the Eventide Court. But I think that's generous enough. Your father has no interest in his old home, or so I believed."

He does, but Fairy Falls matters more.

Clearwater was offering me more than I'd ever believed

he would. There was a catch, there was bound to be, but in the end, he held all the cards, and I held none of them.

"Then I'll surrender." My voice cracked. "Let him go."

"Blair!" Dad shouted.

The hunters closed in around him, blocking him from sight.

Clearwater beckoned to the two hunters holding my arms. "Bring her to the Lancashire Prison for Paranormals."

10

The Lancashire Prison for Paranormals lived up to its reputation. I paced the cell, unable to believe that I was in the very same place in which my dad had spent years of his life. Blank walls greeted me on all sides, with a single door inset with a barred window showing me an equally blank-looking corridor outside. Not a very inspiring sight.

The walls were covered with a spell that stopped my fairy magic working, and I couldn't even fly. I paced instead, anything to keep my thoughts from lingering on the fact that I was here for the long haul. How had my dad managed to stand this for years without going mad?

Imagining him sitting here without complaint, knowing he'd have to keep his secret for my safety and for everyone else… despite it all, I couldn't stop the tears from falling as I sank to the floor. Now that the Inquisitor had taken the Seeing Stone, had it all been for nothing?

I hadn't even been allowed to say goodbye before I'd been hauled off to prison by Clearwater's fairies, where the hunters had been waiting to take me into custody. It was as

I'd feared; Clearwater had total control not only over every single hunter who worked in the top security jail but also over all the local branch leaders, so he didn't even have to pull strings to convince them to lock me up for life.

I scrubbed my eyes with the backs of my hands, anger replacing my grief. I'd surrendered to spare my friends, but would Clearwater genuinely leave them alone while I was locked up and unable to help them? I couldn't count on it. And the knowledge that I could resist the Seeing Stone's power while my dad couldn't bothered me like an itch I couldn't reach. That was the true reason he wanted me out of his sight. I was the one fairy he was unable to control.

As I was pacing the room for what felt like the fiftieth time, the door to my cell clicked open, and Clearwater himself entered. He wore his human glamour, and the Seeing Stone was nowhere in sight. "Well?"

"Well what?" I croaked, wishing he wasn't here to see me crying. "You don't have to pretend to be human, do you? Why the disguise?"

"It's easier this way." He closed the door. "I wanted to see how you were getting on."

I pushed to my feet. "What, have you come to gloat?"

"Not at all," he said. "I was considering allowing you access to a Pixie-Glass. I'm not so heartless that I'd forbid you from contacting your family."

I forced a laugh. "Next, you'll be letting me out on the solstice."

"Did you know I invented that practise just for your father's sake?" he asked. "Few others took me up on the offer. It was all for him and for others of his kind."

"Fairies," I surmised. "You're one too. Why are you still hiding your face? Are you ashamed?"

"Not at all." He studied me. "You're hiding yours too."

"There's no point in using wings in here." Another suspicion pinged inside me. "Unless you think your followers will stab you in the back when your glamour wears off."

"Yet again, you prove that you are far too trusting, Blair," he said. "Not everyone can afford to be as naive as you are."

That's a yes, then. Again, not much use to me in here.

"What's the goal?" I asked. "You have the hunters, and the regional witch council isn't any threat to you either. Are you going after the Head Witches next? Or the werewolves?"

I probably shouldn't have been giving him ideas, but I had the creeping suspicion I knew who he'd target next. He'd explicitly said he wouldn't spare Dad's family, and the other fairies' realms had already been his targets. Because one wasn't enough for him, apparently.

"You think my approach a touch medieval, no doubt, but the fairies have lived like this for a long time," he said. "Our lives are made of conquest. Two kinds of people exist, victor and defeated, and it's possible for one to be both."

"That's a really sad way of looking at the world," I told him. "But I guess what I say doesn't matter to you either way."

In his mind, he was the victor, I was the defeated, and he'd come here for the sole purpose of cementing that victory for himself. And, yes, gloating.

His eyes narrowed a fraction. "It's a shame, Blair. We might have been allies."

"That would never have happened. You know that. You locked up my dad, you had my mother murdered..." My throat closed up. "You should be in my place, but you don't have the heart to see the wrong in what you did."

"Then we'll have to disagree to the end, Blair."

He returned to the door and stepped out into the corridor. I watched him leave, part of me wanting to shout after him, another part wanting to stay quiet and not give him the satisfaction of making me lose my cool.

I had a long stay ahead of me, after all.

————

Time had little meaning while I was inside the cell. I wished I had a clock or a watch or my cat to remind me it was time to feed him. The fact that Sky hadn't walked through the wall said volumes for how secure this place was, but it would have been nice to have company. Sky would never have agreed to be caged, but for all I knew, he was devising a way to get me out at this very moment. He wouldn't give up on me that easily, and neither would my friends, my dad, or Nathan. Would they be able to get me out without drawing Clearwater's wrath, though? Not a chance.

If Clearwater was telling the truth about the Pixie-Glass, my dad and I might be able to talk face-to-face regardless, but how long would that take? Even if I behaved my best, there was no guarantee he'd keep his word. Yet that promise was all I had, and so I clung to the image of my dad's face in the glass as the minutes and hours trickled by.

Clearwater didn't come back, but he sent guards to bring me meals every few hours. They were my only markers of the time passing, and I didn't see a single face I recognised until two days into my captivity.

On the morning of the third day, I woke to the door opening for my morning meal to be delivered. My attention snapped to the guard's face, and I gasped. "You..."

It was Eric, Nathan's brother and Erin's twin.

He ignored me, pushing the door open farther as I scrambled to my feet.

"Eric," I whispered. "Where's your brother? Is he okay?"

Nathan must have been out of his mind with worry. I might have made the right choice, but that didn't mean it hadn't hurt a lot of people, including Nathan.

Still ignoring me, Eric put down the tray of food he'd been sent to deliver.

"Come on, you can tell me that, can't you?" I pressed. "You must know I'm not here because I committed a crime. Clearwater wants me out of the way, and he's not going to let me talk to anyone on the outside."

He backed into the doorway, still not speaking.

Desperation overtook me. "Please—"

"I'm not supposed to talk to you." He pushed the door closed.

"He's not watching you right this instant, is he?" I moved up to the door, my heart racing. "Look, I just want to know he's okay. Nathan."

"He's fine."

True. At least he was being honest.

"And Erin?" My voice caught. "She was worried about you, too, you know."

A pause. "My sister's an idiot."

At least I'd got him to talk rather than ignoring me. "She said the same about you. What's this special mission Clearwater has you doing?"

He gave me an incredulous look. "What on earth makes you think I'd tell *you* that?"

"It's not like I can tell anyone else from in here." *Well, I can if I get the Pixie-Glass. But let's face it, Clearwater won't allow that for a long while, if ever.* "Nobody else is here. You can see that for yourself."

He grunted and turned away. "I don't trust you."

"You're the one with the key and the uniform," I pointed out. "You can't seriously be okay with this. I know he put you under a spell, but—"

His footsteps clacked on the floor as he walked away.

I pushed my face up into the barred window to call after him, "If Nathan is looking for me, can you just tell me that?"

"For both your sakes, I hope he isn't."

Then he was gone.

I moved back from the door, ignoring the tray he'd left me. Eric might have been the least helpful of Nathan's family members, but presumably, his new job involved watching high-security prisoners, and the thought that I had one way to check up on Nathan was a bright light in a week that had otherwise been mired in utter darkness.

And who knew, maybe one day, I'd get through to him.

———

More time passed. I was at the point at which I was miscounting the number of days that had elapsed since I'd been brought in when Eric next walked in to deliver my evening meal.

"Where's your boss?" I asked him without preamble.

He narrowed his eyes and put down the tray. "I'm not supposed to—"

"Talk to me, I know," I said. "He doesn't know we know one another, does he? Or does he not care?"

Eric worked his jaw. "He trusts me."

I wish he didn't. "Erin wanted to trust you too. So did Nathan, but you let both of them down."

Anger flashed in his eyes. Then Eric stepped outside and closed the door on me without another word.

Where is *Clearwater?* I hadn't seen him since that first day, but the other guards wouldn't answer any of my questions. In the absence of any news, my brain conjured up worst-case scenarios, such as Clearwater's armies attacking my dad's home. Or worse, invading Fairy Falls after all.

Unanswered questions ricocheted around my mind as I began yet another pacing circuit of the room. I was acquainted with every inch of my prison by now, having examined it thoroughly for weaknesses like holes in the walls, gaps in the door, anything. No luck. This place was a steel trap.

And yet. On the sixth or seventh day after my imprisonment, I was awoken by a cacophony of voices in the corridor outside. I lifted my head, disoriented, as the voices grew louder, and I glimpsed movement in the corridor.

I moved closer to the door and saw several people in handcuffs walking past. New prisoners? They must have been. Guards walked on either side of their group, and—

My heart skipped a beat. A woman with long, dark hair and a defiant expression walked among the prisoners. *Erin.*

What had she tried to do? Rescue me? I pressed my face against the bars, but she didn't look at me. I didn't recognise any of the other prisoners. As for the guards, Eric didn't appear to be amongst them.

No, that'd be too easy. My hands fisted, part of me fighting the desire to call out to her, for all the good it would do.

A shimmering light reached my eyes, and I recoiled. *Fairy magic.* Was Clearwater back? The light shined over the guards, and my heart climbed into my throat. If I'd been able to use my own magic, I might have been able to tell who the magic belonged to, but I could only watch as the streaming light trickled away, alighting on one of the security guards.

I pressed my face closer to the window again, trying to see the guard the light had appeared to come from. When he tilted his head, our gazes locked, and a gasp lodged in my throat. Despite his human guise, I knew him.

Buck. The shimmering of fairy magic covered his features, but I was sure it was him. He was disguised as a guard. It was a good disguise, too, but it wouldn't fool Clearwater.

"What are you doing?" someone demanded from out of sight. "Stop that at once."

I didn't see who the guard had addressed, but the sound

of thundering footsteps hit my eardrums an instant later. The prisoners scattered, the formation breaking apart into confusion. Only one person remained still—Buck—and this time, when his eyes locked onto mine, he was smiling. Around him, prisoners ran left and right, and within seconds, Erin's face was pressed to the bars of my cell.

"Found her!" she said triumphantly. "Got the key?"

"Sure thing." Buck moved to her side, and moments later, the door to my cell swung open.

"How?" I goggled at the pair of them, lost for words.

"Talk later," Erin replied. "Can you fly?"

Could I? I hadn't been able to sense my fairy magic inside the cell, but Buck had managed to use his, so it must have been possible. I stepped out of the room and was relieved to feel the familiar buzz in my right hand when I snapped my fingers. My wings extended, and relief washed over me like taking in a long breath after being submerged underwater.

Then a prisoner knocked into me, and the effect wore off. Given the pandemonium in here, someone must have unlocked more cells as a diversion unless they always brought that many prisoners in at a time. An alarm began to blare, strident and sharp.

"Yeah. I can fly," I told the others, covering my ears. "But there'll be guards in the way. I can't manoeuvre my wings in here."

"That's why we brought you this." Buck handed me my wand. "And we'll have to move fast. Come on."

"Thank you. Thank you both." I wanted to say more, but not while we were still here in the prison. "Lead the way."

Buck flew ahead, while I let Erin overtake me so I could bring up the rear and glamour any guards who showed up on our tail. Miraculously, none did, probably because they were chasing all the other escaped prisoners and hadn't noticed me slip out of my cell too.

It wasn't until we reached the exit that we found a bottle-neck blocking the way out, guards jammed up against prisoners trying to flee.

Buck snapped his fingers and conjured a dazzling flash of light. He must have been practising, because even I had to squeeze my eyes shut to avoid being blinded. One hand over my eyes, I jabbed my wand at the nearest guards and blasted them with a freeze-frame spell that hit at least one of them.

"Everyone, keep pushing!" Erin told the prisoners.

I geared up to cast another spell.

A guard shouted, "You! Blair Wilkes!"

I panicked and waved my wand, unintentionally conjuring up a waterfall of glitter instead of the spell I'd been intending to cast. That did have the effect of sending the guards recoiling, and the prisoners gained the upper hand enough to shove their way through to the exit.

Buck flew ahead of me, and I kept close behind him as we emerged into the countryside. I exhaled, the fresh air filling my lungs. *Freedom.*

"Hey!" Erin yelled, running to catch up. "Don't leave me down here."

Oops. I'd forgotten she couldn't fly. "How'd you get here? Did the hunters bring you?"

"Yes, and it took bloody forever." She grimaced when Buck lifted her off the ground. "I don't like heights, you know."

"Seriously?" I beat my own wings, alarmed when one of the guards snapped his fingers behind us and a pair of wings extended from his back. *Crap. Some of them are fairies.*

"Let's go!" I pointed my wand at the fairy and cast a spell that knocked him off-balance. Then I launched myself high into the air.

I flew higher, Buck carrying Erin behind me. I didn't want

to leave the other prisoners behind, but they'd wasted no time in scattering in all directions into the forest. I had to trust that they'd find their own way to safety while we made our escape.

"How are the others?" I asked Buck as we flew onward. "Nathan? I'm surprised he didn't volunteer to rescue me."

"He did," Erin told me. "I shot him down. It was too obvious."

"I'm surprised nobody was suspicious that you turned yourself in."

"I didn't," she replied. "I showed up at the prison and let myself get caught. Told them I was there to break you out."

"Did Eric know?"

She went faintly green when a gust of wind hit us in the back. "Honestly, he looked the other way when we walked in. I'm sure he knew Buck wasn't a regular guard."

"Really?"

"Yeah, I'd say so too," Buck said. "I don't like the guy, but I doubt we'd have made it in there without him."

My chest tightened. "Clearwater is going to punish him for this. And I broke my word."

"You didn't think he was actually going to leave Fairy Falls alone, did you?" said Erin. "Come on, Blair."

Well, no. I'd wanted to believe it, but I knew better than to trust a single word Clearwater spoke. "Where is he, though? I haven't seen him in days."

"No clue," Erin answered, "but the reason we got into the jail so easily is because most of his fairies have gone with him."

"Where?" I didn't really need to ask. He must have taken anyone willing to volunteer to join his fairy court and wage war against anyone who would oppose him. "Please tell me he hasn't gone after my dad's family."

"I don't know," Buck replied, "but it's certainly on his list, and considering he has that Seeing Stone, it wouldn't be good news if he did."

No kidding. We might have won one victory, but the question of how to beat an immortal who wielded both a sceptre *and* the Seeing Stone might have been one even Madame Grey couldn't answer.

11

I flew alongside Buck and Erin until we descended through a mass of clouds and found the lake shimmering below.

"This way." Buck swooped down, heading not for Fairy Falls itself but for the hills nearby.

"Aren't we going inside?" I called to him. "Or is the border closed?"

"Not quite yet," said Buck. "We need to make sure Clearwater didn't put any spells on you to trick us or to take down the barriers."

"I didn't think of that," I admitted. "Good point."

On the hillside, several people waited for us. My heart lifted when I saw the familiar faces waiting below for our descent. "Nathan!"

"Blair!"

When I landed, he swept me into his arms briefly before Alissa caught my arm and hugged me too. The next thing I knew, my coworkers had joined her. Even Veronica came running down to hug me too.

"I'm glad you're all right," she said. "Keep still."

"What? Why?" I blinked when she pointed her wand at me. "Wait, what are you all doing out here?"

"Debugging you," said Veronica.

The sensation of water rushing over my head made me gasp, and then it vanished just as quickly. "Did Clearwater put a spell on me?"

"Someone did," said Bethan. "It's all gone now. Don't worry."

"How did you know I was coming… right." I gestured to Erin and Buck, who'd landed nearby. Erin looked considerably relieved to have both her feet back on the ground. "Is everyone okay?"

"In Fairy Falls? Yes." Nathan stepped protectively between me and the others. "Give Blair some space. She's had a rough week or two."

"I have, but why is everyone else here?" They hadn't come solely to greet me, surely. They could have done that on the other side of the barrier, within the safety of Fairy Falls itself.

"Blair," said Veronica, "as much as we would all like to welcome you home after your sojourn in jail, there's another matter that we need to deal with, preferably before Clearwater sends an army on your tail."

I stiffened at the word "army." "What? The fairies? I know Clearwater is going after them."

"Not the fairies," said Nathan. "The witches. Specifically, the coven that created the sceptres."

"What about them?" Disbelief flooded me. "You found them?"

"We did," Bethan put in. "There's one survivor."

Dread rippled down my spine. "Clearwater has the Seeing Stone. Is he going after them next?"

"If he finds out they exist," Veronica put in, "but we'd like to avoid that, wouldn't we?"

"Ideally, yes." I looked from her to my coworkers in

bafflement. "You know where they are? Then how do we stop Clearwater from figuring it out too?"

"He doesn't have the resources we do," Veronica said proudly. "And we're going to lead him on a false trail while you're meeting with the Primrose Coven."

"Why me?" I burst out. "I—I'm not special. I didn't even manage to stop Clearwater from stealing the Seeing Stone—and he doesn't need the sceptre now that he has that."

"I beg to differ." Veronica looked positively excited. "Your father informed me of the *interesting* effects your magic has on the Seeing Stone's capabilities."

Right. The stone didn't affect me, but did that necessarily matter, given his other advantages? "I can't stop the sceptre, though, can I?"

"That's what we're hoping the Primrose Coven will be able to tell us," Bethan ventured. "The trouble is…"

"The trouble is that we aren't the experts," Veronica finished. "But she is."

She pointed towards a middle-aged blond witch who'd been standing so far behind the others that I'd overlooked her altogether. At first, I didn't recognise her face. Then it hit me. "You were at the Head Witches' meeting."

"Correct," said the newcomer. "I am Lady Wildwood, leader of the Wildwood Coven."

But not a Head Witch. No, her daughter had taken that position—much to everyone's shock, or so I'd gathered. "Erm, why are you here? Are you going to speak to the Primrose Coven?"

"Yes," she said. "My coven has our own reasons to want to know more about how we might enable a sceptre to change its wielder."

Did she want her daughter freed from the burden of carrying the sceptre? I knew Robin herself did, though for the time being, she'd resigned herself to the position the same way Rebecca had.

Rebecca. If there was really a way to set her free… "Rebecca isn't coming, though, right?"

"No, it's too risky," said Veronica. "That's why we need someone to travel on her behalf."

"I still don't know why it has to be me." Wasn't Madame Grey a better candidate? Hell, even Blythe was.

"Because you're a fugitive," said Nathan, though he didn't look too happy at the idea of me leaving this soon after my escape from jail. "Clearwater will assume you came straight here. We need to divert his attention."

"Now that we've taken off the tracking spell, it should be easy to lead him astray," Veronica added. "Otherwise, don't you *want* to meet the Primrose Coven?"

"I thought you said there was only one survivor." I turned to Lady Wildwood.

She drew herself upright haughtily. "That's what I'm given to understand," she said. "She's called Adele Primrose. I intended to travel to speak to her alone, but Veronica here *persuaded* me to take you with me. Assuming you aren't going to put us both in danger by mere proximity."

That was nice. "Does your daughter know you're here?"

"No, and I intend to keep it that way." She drew out her wand and gave it a flick, and a broomstick appeared at her feet. "Let's not delay."

I'd been hoping to travel with someone a little friendlier, but it couldn't be helped. I regretfully hugged Nathan goodbye and then got out my wings once more. Lady Wildwood watched with the same stern expression she had worn during our last meeting and then mounted her broomstick. Even that she managed to do with a great deal of poise and elegance, while my wings felt clumsy in comparison.

We flew north—luckily, in the opposite direction to the

LPFP—over the countryside of Cumbria and then further north. After several minutes had passed, I wondered if we might have passed the border to Scotland, but I had no way to tell from up in the air.

Finally, Lady Wildwood dipped near a small cluster of houses that was hardly big enough to be called a village.

"This is the place?" I beat my wings as Lady Wildwood went into a neat and dignified dive towards a house that stood nestled between two hills. Like the Knotgrass Coven's home, it was isolated from its neighbours, separated by a strip of forest and countryside.

I landed on the gravel path in front of the house and snapped my fingers to turn back into my human form. "Does the person we're meeting know we're coming?"

"She does, yes," Lady Wildwood said. "Once I had her contact details, I let her know myself."

She got the details from Veronica, I guess. Lady Wildwood's prim and proper manner stood in stark contrast to that of my excitable boss, but together, they'd managed to find someone who'd been elusive for years.

The witch who came out of the house to greet us was older than I'd expected, around Aveline's age. Her curly grey hair blew sideways in the wind, and she peered at us over a pair of thick half-moon spectacles.

"You're Lady Wildwood, are you?" She addressed the other witch, ignoring me altogether. "I do hope you didn't bring anyone on your tail."

"We weren't followed." She indicated me. "Blair, this is Adele Primrose. Adele, this is Blair Wilkes."

"Wilkes," Adele echoed. "Wilkes isn't a coven name, is it?"

"Ah, no, but you might know the name Wildflower. That was my mother's name." It was a gamble, given that we weren't anywhere near home, but her eyes widened a fraction.

"Interesting. You'd better come in."

We entered the house, which was modestly sized for someone who belonged to such a prestigious coven. The portraits hanging on the walls—all of them depicting witches who looked like younger versions of Adele Primrose herself —were the only clue as to its history. In the older portraits, the witches held sceptres in their hands.

"Go on, ask me your questions," said Adele as we took seats in the plush armchairs in the sitting room. "I have to admit, I'm surprised it's taken this long for one of my coven's sceptres to fall into nonhuman hands."

"How?" I leaned forward in my seat. "I don't understand how Clearwater was able to learn to use a sceptre designed for witches."

"There was a flaw in the design," Adele replied. "My ancestors' fault, of course. They never imagined anyone other than a witch would ever dare to touch one of their sceptres."

"What kind of flaw?" I asked. "It's important. If we can stop him…"

"That's not possible." She drummed her fingers on the arm of her chair. "The flaw is a kind of reset button to return the sceptre to factory settings, as it were. I understand that my ancestors put in the mechanism so that the sceptre could be unbound from an unsuitable owner if such a situation arose."

My heart lurched in my chest. "Does that mean it's possible to unbind it from him?"

"It *is* unbound," she said. "Anyone who holds that sceptre has an equal chance of wielding its power."

My mouth fell open. Clearwater wasn't special. He'd taken the sceptre and undone the magic binding it to its wielder.

"That's not what you implied when we spoke earlier,"

Lady Wildwood said haughtily. "I thought the flaw was designed to unbind the sceptre from a specific wielder, not to enable *anyone* to use it."

"The sceptres were designed to pick their own wielders," said Adele. "I don't advise you to undo the spells on every single sceptre, even if I were able to tell you how to do it. Which I can't. My ancestors took that secret to their graves."

"How'd Clearwater figure it out?" I wondered.

"I imagine an immortal fairy ruler has magic at his disposal that the rest of us can merely dream of." She shook her head. "Unlike fairies, however, we humans age, and I have little interest in getting involved in another battle."

"You don't have to," Lady Wildwood told her. "However, we would appreciate your advice on how to handle the sceptres. Both of us know people who were chosen against their will."

Adele turned to my companion. "I understand that you want your daughter freed from the burden, but you must know that breaking the sceptre's magic would lead to more trouble than you desire."

"I gathered," said Lady Wildwood. "Is the only option to wait for Samhain and try again?"

"Correct," she said. "There's a reason my ancestors bound all sceptres to obey one person at a time."

My chest tightened. "Another sceptre is bound to a friend of mine. She's only eleven. Didn't you put age restrictions on the spell?"

She gave a soft, incredulous laugh. "No. Eleven is old enough to wield a wand, isn't it?"

"It's too young to be saddled with the responsibility that comes with being a Head Witch," I objected. "Her mother is a nasty piece of work and has been trying to kidnap her ever since she claimed the sceptre. She's also distantly related to my mother's coven. To the Wildflowers."

"Really," she said. "How long has she held the sceptre?"

"Since Samhain, but—"

"Then surely, you can wait four months until the next."

"Not when our town's practically under siege." My hands clenched. "I'm sorry. I just… you mean to say there's no way to undo the binding?"

"No." She eyed the portraits on her wall. "For better or worse, I'm the last of my coven, and I have no trace of the gift myself."

"Then we have to destroy Clearwater's sceptre to keep it out of his hands." I glanced at Lady Wildwood, whose own expression was perturbed. "Or steal it."

"The sceptre cannot be destroyed," Adele said. "My ancestors thought of everything, and if it was possible to destroy a sceptre, someone would have already succeeded."

"They might have," I said. "I don't know anything about your ancestors. How did you end up being the only one left?"

"Wand-making covens have a tendency to make powerful enemies," she said. "I'm perfectly fine with the line ending with me. Not everything has to last forever."

Tell that to the immortal fairies.

Stealing the sceptre was an option, certainly, but Clearwater had the Seeing Stone. With that, he'd see us coming no matter what we did.

"In that case, we'll wait for Samhain," said Lady Wildwood. "How exactly did your ancestors ensure the wrong person wasn't chosen? Is there a way to manipulate the choice, short of keeping anyone out of the room who might use the sceptre for evil?"

"You might try offering the sceptre a different selection," said Adele. "Rather than the same few witches or covens."

Huh? "Can you do that? Offer the sceptre to other witches who aren't in the covens?"

"Of course," she said. "If it wasn't possible for anyone to

wield a sceptre, your fairy wouldn't have taken one for his own, would he?"

She had a point. The sceptre had chosen Rebecca because she'd been there at the time, but there'd only been a handful of alternatives. *I wonder...*

"That's all I have," Adele added. "I do trust you'll come up with a solution to your dilemma."

"Thank you for talking to us." Lady Wildwood rose elegantly to her feet. "This was illuminating."

"Yeah, thanks." It wasn't the outcome I'd hoped for, but she'd given us some information we might be able to use in our fight against Clearwater.

Adele led us to the doors, and we walked out onto the gravel path. The open space and cold breeze made me aware of how far beyond the boundaries of Fairy Falls we'd travelled. I could only hope that Veronica and my coworkers had concocted enough of a distraction that Clearwater hadn't figured out where we'd gone.

"Your daughter can wait until Samhain, right?" I asked Lady Wildwood as she mounted her broomstick. "I guess she won't be happy, but that can't be helped."

"She won't," she agreed, "but she needs to accept that waiting is the only option. As for your friend..."

"Rebecca." I grimaced. "She'd be fine with waiting if not for her mother. Mrs Dailey almost bewitched her into walking straight to her side once already. And what if her mother realises that she could just snatch up the sceptre and use it herself?"

"Not without undoing its magic," she said. "Like Clearwater did."

True. I didn't know if Clearwater would be willing to do the same for his erstwhile ally, but I'd think on that later. Meanwhile, I snapped my fingers and turned into fairy mode to fly home.

The journey passed in a blur of exhaustion, and I didn't realise just how tired I was until I finally landed outside Fairy Falls and my knees buckled beneath me.

"Blair." Nathan was at my side in an instant, taking my arm. "Are you okay?"

"Yeah. It's been a long day." I looked around, seeing that Veronica and the others had departed. Only Nathan had remained outside the border, waiting for me. My eyes stung with tears, and I threw myself on him with a sob.

"Ow, Blair," he said, his voice muffled. "You're squeezing the life out of me."

"Sorry." I loosened my hold. "I missed you. While I was in jail, I mean."

"Same here." His gaze softened. "I was going out of my mind with worry. My sister had to talk me out of going after you a dozen times."

"I figured." I swallowed hard. "I'm surprised you let her go in your place. And Buck too."

"She rightly pointed out that Buck was more likely than anyone else to be able to get into the jail without tripping any alarms. The people in there are used to being bewitched by fairies."

"True enough." As we crossed the boundary to Fairy Falls, more thoughts came crashing into my mind. "I need to talk to Madame Grey and Rebecca."

"That can wait," he said firmly. "You need rest and recuperation."

"I know, but I ought to at least let everyone know I'm okay." Such as… "Oh god. My foster parents. They'll have been mad with worry too."

Worse, I hadn't been around to shield them from the worst of the magical world. After all the work I'd done, carefully easing them into my new life, anything might have happened in my absence. Granted, they'd already seen my cat transform into a giant monster to pin down an intruder and hadn't run screaming in terror, but still.

"Don't worry. Your father's been taking care of them," Nathan said. "I should have told you earlier. Sorry."

"My dad?" I gaped at him. "What? They know he's a fairy?"

"If they do, I'm sure it's fine, Blair."

"No, it isn't." Alarm blared through my mind. With my tiredness forgotten, I flew down the street towards home. It was still the middle of the day, evidenced by the people out on their lunch breaks who stared at me as I flew past.

Nathan hurried in behind me. "I'll tell Madame Grey you're back. Really, though, you need to rest. You've had a long day."

"I know." I wanted to go home with him and forget all my responsibilities, but I'd have been the worst daughter on the planet if I left my foster parents to find out the truth secondhand. "I need to talk to them, though. See you in a bit?"

"Of course." He brushed a kiss to my lips and then went into the witches' headquarters.

I continued to fly towards home. At the door, I was greeted by a fluffy boulder crashing into my chest.

"Sky." I yelped when he dug his claws in. "Ow!"

"MIAOW," he admonished, hopping out of my arms and herding me towards the front door.

"Sorry I got jailed." I followed him inside, where the flat door nudged open.

Alissa bounded into view. "Blair!" She rushed to greet me. "I'm glad you're okay. Bethan told me you went off on an errand, but I was worried."

"I'm fine." I peered behind her, seeing that the living room was empty. "Wait, where are my foster parents?"

"Your dad took them out," she said. "He's been doing his

best to keep them occupied, but it was hard for them to avoid guessing you were in some kind of trouble."

"So they're okay?" Presumably, he hadn't told them he was a fairy, then. He wouldn't be able to hide the truth forever, but maybe I had some chance of salvaging this after all. "I'll go and find them."

"Now?" she asked. "If you're sure, but you look exhausted."

"I need a cloning spell." I rubbed my forehead. "Where'd he take them, do you know?"

"Miaow," Sky piped up.

I swivelled to him. "You know where they are?"

"I bet he does." Alissa grinned and backed into the flat. "Let me know how it goes."

"Sure thing." I tripped over Sky on the way out, as he insisted on walking close enough to my feet to be in danger of getting kicked. "Sky, I can't walk *or* fly with you clinging to me like that."

"Miaow." He gave me a few inches of distance and beckoned with his tail.

"Did you try to rescue me from prison?" I asked curiously, following his lead. This time, I used my Seven Millimetre Boots to fly, not my wings. If my foster parents hadn't seen my dad's real face yet, I didn't need to undo his hard work by exposing my wings immediately. "They fairy-magic-proofed the cell."

"Miaow," Sky replied, bounding along at my side.

"Or were you watching my foster parents instead?" I guessed. "I can't believe they lasted a week here without me without losing their sanity."

When we reached the lake, I was greeted by the improbable sight of my dad and my foster parents sitting on the bank of the lake on... was that a picnic blanket?

"Dad." I stared, nonplussed. "What are you doing out here?"

"Blair." Dad flew to me and wrapped his arms around me, while my foster parents exclaimed behind him. "You're okay."

"Yeah. I'm sorry I didn't come back straight away." I hugged each of my foster parents in turn next and then reached down to pet Sky before he got jealous. "I got diverted. Long story."

"Your father told us some of it," said Mrs Wilkes, returning to the picnic blanket. "Come here. You must be starving."

I was. My last meal had been the previous night, in jail, and the basket of carefully prepared food nearly made me start bawling. "You knew I was coming back today?"

"Your boyfriend told us," Mr Wilkes said. "Is it true that you were held captive?"

I might have concocted a lie, but after the day I'd had, I had no ideas left in me but the truth. "I got jailed by a megalomaniacal fairy."

When both of them goggled at me, I backtracked. "Ah, have you heard about fairies yet?"

"Yes," my dad answered. "I told them what I am."

I lifted my head, surveying my foster parents. They looked worried but not as if they were traumatised from their last encounter with the fairies. "But what about…?"

"I thought there were some things you could explain yourself, Blair," Dad said, "but they already guessed I wasn't human, and it was easier to tell the truth."

Evidently, he hadn't told them about the last time they'd met the fairies. That could wait until later, but for now, I took in a deep breath and snapped my fingers. My wings unfurled behind my back, and both Mr and Mrs Wilkes gasped.

"This is me." My voice shook a little, but my imprisonment had drained a lot of my fear. "I'm half fairy. As you probably guessed, since my dad is a fairy, and we're related—"

"They're yours, Blair?" Mr Wilkes stared at the wings. "Remarkable."

I shifted on my feet, uncomfortable. "I can put them away."

"No, they suit you," said Mrs Wilkes. "Don't they?"

"Of course they do," said Mr Wilkes. "You can fly? Really? You have to tell us all about it."

My eyes stung with relieved tears at the knowledge that my foster parents accepted me, wings and all.

Whatever came next, at least I had that.

12

I spent the rest of the afternoon with my dad and foster parents, catching up on the time we'd missed. For a brief while, I could pretend the world outside didn't exist, while gradually, the sun dipped in the sky, light playing on the vibrant waters of the lake. All too soon, responsibility called. Alissa texted me, letting me know that her grandmother wanted to talk to me, and I figured Nathan had only been able to stall her for so long. She'd want the full story from me, both of my escape from prison and of my meeting with Adele Primrose.

I parted ways with my foster parents outside the witches' headquarters, trusting Sky to guide them home. My familiar had taken my last command to heart, and while I would have been glad of his company while I'd been in jail, I doubted Mr and Mrs Wilkes would have got through the past couple of weeks with their sanity intact if not for him and my dad.

Madame Grey waited for me inside the lobby, where she beckoned me into a classroom. "Rebecca's at school. I'm assuming you don't have a way to change her sceptre's allegiance?"

"I don't." Guilt bubbled up inside me. "We can't take the sceptre from her before Samhain, not without breaking it the way Clearwater did—which would enable anyone else who picked up the sceptre to use it too."

"I see." She studied me for a moment. "I was afraid it would be something like that."

"You knew?"

"I suspected," she said. "Wands are similar. Once claimed, they rarely switch to a new user unless the creator uses a spell that resets the wand altogether."

"Clearwater must have found a way to do the same to a sceptre without consulting the coven," I explained. "Adele Primrose doesn't have the gift."

"I know, Blair," she said. "I gather the fairies have magic at their disposal that the covens do not, but the reverse is also true. I hear you were able to resist the Seeing Stone, for instance."

"I was." I dropped my gaze. "The council... did they all die?"

"No, they didn't," she replied. "Those who were present at the location of the Seeing Stone fled upon Clearwater's intrusion."

"Why?" My hands curled into fists. "Didn't they even put up a fight?"

"Clearwater brought an army with him," she said. "They didn't have time to gather one of their own, and there was no sense in sacrificing their lives."

"They aren't the ones who the Seeing Stone can control, though," I pointed out. "The fairies are."

I hadn't asked my dad if he'd heard from his sister yet, but she must have been on his mind too. Clearwater hadn't found his way into her home, but with the Seeing Stone in his hands, even the formidable Lady Eventide wouldn't be able to stand against him.

"The regional witch council is formulating a plan," she said. "We're in contact. However, we'll need your help, Blair. Taking the Seeing Stone back will depend upon someone who can get close to him without falling under its spell."

"What about the sceptre?" I asked. "The sceptre isn't under his control, not exclusively. If we were able to steal it back, any of us could use it."

"The sceptre is unpredictable," she said. "For now, I would like you to rest, Blair. You've done enough today."

Protests rose to my tongue, but she was right. I was exhausted, my mind rattled by the new revelations, and I needed time to think.

Then, with the others' help, I might be able to come up with a solution that would enable us to take Clearwater down without any more people having to die.

———

The following day, I woke up incredibly well rested, having slept like a log with Sky purring on my feet and Nathan at my side.

Upon seeing my eyes were open, Nathan kissed me lightly. "What's the plan for today?"

"Figure out how to depose a world-conquering fairy with two impossible-to-beat weapons." I gave a laugh. "So, the usual."

"Yeah." His smile faded. "I wish I knew."

We'd briefly discussed potential plans at the pub yesterday evening, but since my foster parents had been there, I hadn't wanted to go into too much detail. My parents had tried to join in, and their idea of dropping a truck on Clearwater's head admittedly had merit, but I had little doubt that he'd have defences against such mundane weapons.

"Maybe the other fairies can shed some light," I remarked.

"I haven't talked to them since I got back, and I haven't asked my dad if he's heard from his sister, either."

"There's time," said Nathan. "You don't need to worry about everyone else."

"But I didn't keep my end of the bargain with Clearwater," I said. "That means he's likely to strike against us or against my dad's family. If he isn't putting all his efforts into finding me, that is."

Veronica had set up an elaborate false trail across half the country, according to Madame Grey, so that ought to keep him busy for a while. But there was still Mrs Dailey to consider, and she was no doubt watching like a hawk for another opportunity to sneak in and claim her youngest daughter.

"There'll be a solution somewhere, I'm sure," Nathan said. "One that doesn't involve you risking your life."

Sky growled agreement while I slumped against the pillow. "I get it. I don't much like the idea of being locked up again, either, but he tried to control me—Clearwater did—and it didn't work. How many other fairies are immune to the Seeing Stone?"

"You can't take down a one-man army, least of all when he has an actual army too." Nathan gently stroked my hair. "You don't need to take the weight of the world on your shoulders, either. Madame Grey is talking to the council about getting the Seeing Stone back, isn't she?"

"They can't go into the fairies' realm," I mumbled. "Neither can anyone else except my dad, and—"

And Blythe had the portal that led directly into Clearwater's realm, but it didn't work any longer.

"Relax." He kissed me again. "I have to report to Steve. He won't be happy at the increased risk of an attack."

"Great." I dragged myself out of bed. "Let me guess: he's looking for a way to blame it on me."

"Actually, I think he blames your father instead," Nathan replied. "Your dad refused to tell Steve the details of what happened between you and Clearwater when he captured you."

"I bet Steve loved that." I could just picture the grumpy gargoyle ranting and raving about my dad being an obstructionist, though if anyone asked me, Steve ought to have been grateful that he'd at least had me out of his hair while I'd been in jail. "Has anyone told him about our visit to the Primrose Coven yet?"

"Yes, but you know the covens aren't of any interest to him," Nathan said. "Like I said, don't stress yourself out. A solution will come when you aren't thinking about it."

"Yeah."

But will it come before Clearwater attacks? That was the question that plagued me as I went to shower and get dressed —abetted by Sky, who seemed to object to me wearing socks —and then left Nathan's house.

Alissa had sent a message asking if I wanted to meet up at Charms & Caffeine, which seemed like an excellent idea. I bought a muffin and coffee for breakfast, and the two of us chatted about mundane subjects, happy to make the most of the haven of ordinariness amid the chaos that otherwise made up my life.

Partway through, the café door opened, and a tall Black man glided in, smiling at Alissa with pointed teeth.

"Oh, hey, Samuel." She waved her boyfriend over. "I didn't know you were coming."

"I had a free hour, and I thought I'd come to check up on Blair." He eyed me. "You don't look any worse for wear after your ordeal."

"Erm, thanks." There weren't any free chairs, and when he hovered next to the table to talk to Alissa, I abruptly felt like a third wheel. "How's the library?"

"Spectacular," he said. "My new assistant has been a great help."

"Good." A thought occurred to me. "Have you seen Vincent recently?"

"I expect he's around," said Samuel. "Might I ask why?"

I shrugged. "I was curious if he had questions, assuming my cat didn't tell him everything already."

Might he have ever met the Primrose Coven himself, for instance? I was conscious that this was too public a setting to discuss the subject, and I didn't need the whole town to find out that it was possible to break a sceptre's bond with its witch. It was unlikely that anyone else would figure out how to do whatever Clearwater had done, but Rebecca's standing as Head Witch was precarious enough already.

"I also wondered if he might have an idea about how to deal with our fairy nemesis," I added when Samuel gave me a sceptical look. "I should probably ask him that myself, though. Is he at home?"

"He might be." The vampire angled himself towards the door. "I can tell him you'd like to meet with him if I see him."

"Nah, it's fine," I reassured him. "You can have my seat. Alissa, I'll see you later?"

"Of course."

We both waved goodbye to Layla behind the counter before leaving the cafe.

I'd initially thought the most likely place to find the vampire was his own house, but when I left the cafe, I found my attention captured by the local bookshop where I'd first met him. On impulse, I darted inside, and part of me was unsurprised when I saw Vincent standing amongst the shelves. The pale, elegant vampire also looked unsurprised to see me—as did Sky, who sat at his feet, purring away. Why my cat was so fond of the vampire, I hadn't the faintest idea.

"Oh, hello, Blair," Vincent said. "Enjoy your trip?"

"Are you really asking if I enjoyed being incarcerated?" I asked incredulously. *Vampires.* "Of course not."

"I meant your visit to the Primrose Coven."

"Oh." Oops. "I guess it was enlightening."

"Indeed?" He arched a brow. "If you want to know if I was aware of the Primrose Coven's location, I was not. They've been in hiding for centuries."

"Right." It didn't matter if he'd known, I supposed, given that the Primrose Coven hadn't been able to help with Rebecca's dilemma. "I guess you know the sceptre isn't bound to Clearwater."

"Nor to anyone else," he agreed. "Though I also imagine that fairy who looked after the Seeing Stone for years is quite irate at Clearwater for stealing it back."

Oh, no. Conor. I'd utterly forgotten that Conor, who'd held the Seeing Stone inside his own house on behalf of my dad while he'd been in jail, might not be particularly happy with the witches for letting the Stone fall into Clearwater's hands.

"I haven't seen him yet." I dragged my thoughts back to the reason I'd wanted to speak to Vincent in the first place. "But I wondered if you had any ideas about how to handle Clearwater. I'm trying to come up with a plan to get the Seeing Stone and the sceptre away from him, but I'm drawing a blank."

He crouched and stroked Sky behind the ears. "Now, what makes you think I would know any better?"

"You're the oldest vampire in town," I pointed out. "Haven't you lived a long enough life that you've faced pretty much any possible scenario?"

"Such as a fairy stealing a Seeing Stone?" He shook his head. "*That,* I hadn't experienced until I met you, Blair. You do have a habit of stirring up new and exciting kinds of trouble."

"Thanks." I wasn't entirely sure if he meant that as a compliment. "Does it have any weaknesses?"

"Which, the Seeing Stone or the sceptre?" he asked. "Both do, as does Clearwater himself. I imagine the other fairies would know more of the latter than I do."

"I guess." I suppressed a sigh. "You'd tell me if you knew how to win this, wouldn't you?"

"Of course I would." He tutted. "Blair, you need to have more faith in those who seek to protect you."

"Miaow." Sky nudged me in the leg.

"What?" I crouched down and stroked him behind the ears. "Sky, help me out here. What's Clearwater's weakness? No, never mind. You're a cat."

"An astute observation," the vampire said. "I shall see you later, Blair."

As he vanished, I rolled my eyes. "I *hope* he meant that in a general sense this time. We don't need any more intruders."

"Miaow," Sky agreed. At least he'd stayed with me instead of following Vincent, but if the vampire hadn't figured out a way to stop Clearwater, who would?

More to the point, he'd given me another dilemma: namely Conor and how he might react to the news that the Seeing Stone was in the enemy's hands. My dad would surely have told him already, but it was worth checking.

I left the bookstore with Sky on my heels. Despite the lingering sense of impending doom, it was nice to walk through Fairy Falls's streets in the late morning when nobody else was out. I savoured the cool breeze on my face and the sounds of birdsong that greeted me when I entered the forest, while in the background came the soft noise of the waterfall.

Once I'd found the path to the fairies' part of the forest, I brought out my wings and flew to the clearing.

I knocked on the door to my dad's cottage, and he answered with a smile. "Blair."

"Hey, Dad." I followed him into the cottage, where Sky climbed onto the sofa to claim his usual spot. "I have a question. Does Conor know about the Seeing Stone?"

His face fell. "Yes. He flew into a terrible rage when I told him, and I haven't seen him since."

I grimaced. "Yeah. I figured he'd react badly, but I kind of forgot until Vincent reminded me."

Dad's brows rose. "You met with the vampire?"

"I hoped he might be able to help me figure out how to beat Clearwater," I explained, "but he said the answers were more likely to be with the fairies."

"Did he now?" He paused. "Clearwater is unique among the fairies, though he does share some of our weaknesses. Iron, for instance."

"Iron," I repeated. "What, am I supposed to wave a sword at him until he drops the Seeing Stone?"

"That's one possible strategy, but Clearwater will no doubt have taken that obvious weakness into account."

"True, and it'd have to be a human who did it," I added. "Not a fairy. Or a half fairy. I'm okay near iron, aren't I?"

"Iron doesn't have the same effect on half fairies, so you'd be fine," he said. "However, the Seeing Stone will warn him of any oncoming threat, so it's possible that he'll be expecting us to try exactly that."

"That and, you know, I don't have a sword." I gave a wry smile. "We could always try my foster parents' idea of dropping a truck on his head. Would the Seeing Stone help him see *that* coming?"

"Miaow," said Sky.

"That probably means he thinks I'm losing my grip," I added.

Sky stood up and stretched, arching his back.

"Which I might be, but I did just spend over a week locked in a high-security prison. Clearwater wasn't even around for most of that time."

"Really?" Dad asked. "I wonder what he was doing. Scheming in his own realm, I assume."

"Yeah." I fidgeted, conscious that he might be plotting to get me back into his clutches at any instant. "And your sister? He can't get into *her* realm?"

"No," he said. "He can't. Remember that even I needed an invitation directly from my sister to get into her home. At one time, the courts were able to freely invade one another's domains, but these days, every realm has employed powerful magical defences to keep out intruders. My sister is no exception."

"Good." If the fairies had an equivalent to the defensive spell Rebecca had cast around Fairy Falls, it might keep Clearwater at bay. For now.

My dad leaned forward in his seat. "I wonder if we should check on Conor. He might have some ideas as to how to deal with Clearwater."

"Does he even know I'm back?" I didn't much like the idea of putting myself in range of Conor's temper, but at least my dad would be with me.

"That's a good question." Dad got to his feet. "We'll see."

I gave Sky a stroke and left him curled up on the sofa as I followed my dad out of the house.

From there, the pair of us made our way out of the clearing. Conor lived at the farthest end of the path, apart from the other fairies and humans alike. Nestled between the trees, his small cottage held the same abandoned air as it had the first time I'd visited.

Dad walked up to the front gate and pushed it inward, and I followed him to the front door. The curtains were drawn, and nobody answered his knock.

My spine prickled. "Might he have gone out?"

"He rarely does if he can help it." He hesitated then snapped his fingers, causing the door to swing inward.

I hovered on the threshold, not wanting to follow him in, but the musty smell within suggested nobody had been here in days. Oh crap. Conor hadn't gone to fight Clearwater solo, had he?

Dad's grim expression when he met me at the door told me he suspected the same. "I'll ask the other fairies if they've seen him, but he always keeps to himself."

"Yeah. And if the last time you saw him was when he got mad about the Seeing Stone…" I trailed off, not wanting to assume the worst, but I didn't know Conor as well as my dad did.

We retraced our flight path to the clearing in grim silence.

Partway there, we encountered a pair of fairies on the path. Rosalyn and Ani flew side by side as if running an errand.

"Hey, Blair." Rosalyn gave me a strained smile in greeting. "Are you okay? I heard about Clearwater capturing you."

"I think he went easy on me, considering," I replied. "I have a question. Have either of you seen Conor?"

"No, not recently," she said. "Not that I remember, anyway."

Ani shook her head too. "No, nor me. Why?"

Something about her tone made me pause. "He seems to have left his house. My dad and I were concerned about him. When did you last see him?"

"Hmm, a while ago," Rosalyn said. "Before you left."

Lie. As the truth rang in my ears, I stared at her. Why would she lie to me?

"Blair?" Ani asked. "Is something wrong?"

"No. Yes." The other fairies didn't know I could sense lies.

It only worked on the half humans, but if she was being less than honest… "I think he might have gone after Clearwater."

Alarm flickered in Rosalyn's eyes. "He didn't, did he?"

"Yeah, that's why I need to know where he's been in the past few days," I explained. "He's angry about the loss of the Seeing Stone. And it wouldn't surprise me if he'd gone to steal it back."

"Oh no." She covered her face. "I'm sorry."

"What?" Ani looked to her friend in confusion. "He hasn't left town, has he?"

Rosalyn nodded. "I did see him leaving the forest a couple of days ago, but when he saw me, he asked me not to tell anyone. I didn't realise he might be going there."

True. "Thanks for letting me know anyway."

If he'd gone after Clearwater, it might be too late already, and Dad's bleak expression suggested the same.

"It's just like him to sneak off without my knowing," he muttered. "This isn't good. With the Seeing Stone…"

"Clearwater can control any fairy, I know." I took in a breath. "But where *is* Clearwater at the moment? If he's in his own realm, Conor can't go after him, can he?"

"No," said Dad, "but if Clearwater is looking for his escaped prisoner…"

Oh. Oh no.

"Blair!" Someone shouted my name.

I spun around, seeing Ani flying back towards us at speed.

"Ani?" I called back. "What's wrong?"

"Those hunters." She pointed over her shoulder. "They're back."

"What?" I beat my wings as I turned around in midair. "Where?"

"Near the lake." She flew higher, above the treetops, and pointed over the forest towards the expanse of water.

As Dad and I rose to join her, I spied several figures on the shore of the lake, right beside the border.

"They have some nerve." I kept both eyes on the hunters as I flew towards them, recognising Sleepy's, Dopey's, and Grumpy's faces. *They're here for Rebecca, I bet.*

Except this time, they weren't alone. Someone else stood beside the three hunters, and it wasn't Mrs Dailey or a human.

"Conor," Dad whispered, his gaze fixed on the winged figure behind the three hunters. "What…?"

"Don't go any closer." I caught my dad's arm as he made to fly over to his friend. Conor's expression showed no signs of recognition at our approach. "He's under Clearwater's spell."

Clearwater must have used the Seeing Stone on Conor. And now he'd brought the enemy to our doorstep.

13

onor's expression remained blank as we descended, while the three hunters smirked at me. *Is Mrs Dailey here? Or Clearwater? Surely not—he has better allies than Sleepy, Dopey and Grumpy—but Conor is under his spell. He has to be.*

"Conor!" Dad called to his friend. "Come to your senses. He's controlling you."

Conor lifted his head, and my heart gave a sickening dive when he beat his wings and launched into flight—straight through the barrier and into Fairy Falls.

He was an ally, an inhabitant of Fairy Falls, and the defences had recognised him as such and let him in.

"Conor!" I shouted at him. "Fight off his control!"

The three hunters laughed uproariously, but I ignored them. Was there any way to undo what Clearwater had done? As the Seeing Stone wasn't present, I thought the effects would be less powerful, but Conor showed no signs of having heard me. He came to a halt in midair and raised a hand.

"Blair!" My dad shouted a warning as a bolt of lightning came plunging towards me.

I dropped in flight, narrowly missing being struck. The air tingled with static, and I snapped my fingers, calling upon my own magic.

"Snap out of it!" I called to Conor. "You must remember who you are. He's brainwashed you."

The question was, had Clearwater ordered him to bring me in dead or alive? I didn't know, but that magic of his was serious business. Another bolt of lightning struck the ground nearby, leaving a sizzling patch in the grass.

"Conor." My dad flew at him, ignoring my warning, and tackled the other fairy. The two grappled, sparks flying, while I flew below them, trying to figure out how to help my dad without putting myself into the line of fire.

As I hovered, torn, someone seized one of my wings. The attack startled me so much that I lost my balance, my feet skimming the ground, and Grumpy seized the other wing too.

"Hey!" I twisted, trying to free myself. "You're not supposed to be in—"

Oh no. The barrier. I'd been too fixated on Conor to notice I'd flown right out of range of Fairy Falls's defences, and now, Grumpy held my wings in his meaty fists, preventing me from getting free.

He bared his teeth in a grin. "You can stay here until the Head Witch comes to your rescue."

Rebecca. He wanted to use me to lure Rebecca out. And with my dad occupied fighting Conor, he might just get his wish.

"I don't need to be rescued."

I gasped when a fist slammed into my cheek. The sudden sharp pain startled me, and I was too slow to stop Sleepy from grabbing my wand.

Ow. My face throbbed. I tried to lunge at Sleepy, but Grumpy held me back, gripping my wings in both hands, leaving me flailing desperately.

"Blair!" My dad shouted my name, breaking away from Conor.

"Dad!" I made to snap my fingers, but Grumpy got there first, releasing one wing and seizing my wrist instead. Pain ricocheted up my arm when he moved his grip to my fingers, preventing me from calling upon my fairy magic.

Dad, meanwhile, continued to fly towards me, not noticing that Conor was fast on his heels, hand raised for the kill.

No.

Magic arced through the air and knocked Conor out of the sky. He hit the ground, landing in a statue-like pose that could only be the result of a freeze-frame spell. A powerful one.

"No." I gasped, trying to break out of the hunters' hold, but they hadn't released me even when their ally had fallen.

Instead, the hunters' attention was fixed on the person who'd cast the spell. *Rebecca.* She marched towards me, her sceptre in her hand.

"Let go of her!" she shouted at the hunters.

"Rebecca, don't." Where was Madame Grey? And Blythe? I could only assume that Rebecca had seen the flashes of light and come to investigate for herself, but she knew what would happen if she left the safety of Fairy Falls. "Rebecca!"

Rebecca took one step forward, and a muffled blast went off. She shouted in alarm, the sound lost in the din of the explosion, while clouds of billowing smoke prevented me from seeing my surroundings. *What in the hell was that?*

I coughed, squinting through the haze, but even the purple glow of Rebecca's sceptre was lost to sight, and the ringing in my ears from the blast prevented me from hearing anything else.

"Rebecca!" I shouted. "Dad!"

"Quiet, you." Grumpy growled from behind me. "Or else we'll take you to Mrs Dailey as well."

"You aren't taking Rebecca, either." I squirmed in his grip, scanning the smoke for her. *Rebecca.*

"Your choice." Grumpy's voice receded as he let me go— and in his place, a net came down on my head.

"Hey!" I flailed, stickiness pressing against me from all angles as if I was caught in a massive spiderweb. *It's one of those hunter nets.* I'd forgotten how inescapable their enhanced nets were, and no matter how hard I tried, I couldn't break free.

"Mrs Dailey is going to reward us handsomely for this!" crowed Grumpy, sounding uncharacteristically gleeful. "And *you* won't get in our way, Blair Wilkes."

"Let me go!" The smoke cleared a little, and my heart lurched. A second net lay on the ground nearby, and a pair of panicked eyes stared at me from beneath the weblike substance. *Rebecca.*

"Blair!" My dad's voice shouted from above, but the net prevented me from seeing his location. "Let her go."

"We'll do worse to her if you come any closer," Grumpy called to him. "Get lost, fairy."

"Should we take him too?" asked Dopey.

"No need," said Sleepy. "She's here."

A thrill of dread raced through my veins, and a gust of wind swept the rest of the smoke away. When it cleared, a familiar voice spoke. "So you three are good for something after all."

"You," my dad said. "Stay away from my daughter."

"I'm here for *my* daughter," said Mrs Dailey. "I'd suggest you leave."

Dad. A light burned my eyes, forcing me to close them. Mrs Dailey had cast a spell, and I could only hope that my dad had moved out of the way in time.

"That's better," she said. "I'll take my daughter back now."

"No!" With a frantic scream, I flung myself at the net, but a shock rang through my nerves, and the world went black.

———

This time, I opened my eyes not to a prison cell but to a small room containing two chairs and little else. Despite the lack of furnishings, I knew where I was: the Knotgrass Coven's house. Or rather, Mrs Dailey's new home.

I pushed to my knees with difficulty. My limbs were clumsy and slow. Someone had removed the net, a small mercy, but its aftershocks had left me unable to stand without my knees giving way. Waving goodbye to dignity, I dragged myself on my knees to a chair and fell into it a moment before the door opened and Mrs Dailey herself entered the room.

"Good, you're awake." She closed the door behind her. "I wondered if that net was laced with too strong a dose of poison."

"Poison!" I croaked, belatedly realising that I was still in my fairy form. No wonder I felt so unbalanced. My wings... I couldn't feel them. They'd gone completely numb.

"A mild one," Mrs Dailey said with a pleasant smile as if we were meeting over coffee and not in a prison. "I'd advise you not to try to escape. Every inch of this place is protected."

I'd expected as much. "Have you locked your daughter up too?"

"No," she said. "Rebecca has been given the chance to prove herself loyal to me."

I jerked in my seat as if she'd slapped me. "Did you wipe her memories like you promised?"

"No," she said. "I didn't. Believe it or not, I'm capable of restraint, Blair, and I would only use that power on someone who isn't worth trying to convince."

"Meaning me." Fear trickled down my spine at the knowledge that I hadn't a hope of outrunning her in this state.

"Once, yes," she said. "However, I wouldn't want to deprive Prince Clearwater of his vengeance upon you and risk incurring his wrath by taking away his prize."

Clearwater. "He gave Conor to you to lure me out of town, didn't he?"

"The fairy?" She pursed her lips. "Yes, he did. I imagine Clearwater will be able to undo what my daughter did to him."

Huh? Oh, right, Rebecca had used her sceptre to turn Conor into a statue. And my dad… "Is my dad okay?"

"Assuming he hasn't been foolish enough to follow you here, I imagine he is."

Good to know. "You're giving me to Clearwater. When is he coming?"

Mrs Dailey arched a brow. "Are you so keen to be sent to your fate?"

No. I want to know what Clearwater is doing. Not that it made a difference given my current position. "Unless he isn't here. Unless…"

He's attacking my dad's family.

A smile curled her mouth at the sight of the horror in my eyes. "Unless he's taking what is owed to him."

"Doesn't he already have one fairy court?" I asked desperately. "Why does he need another?"

"Oh." Pity entered her eyes. "You think I meant the sorry excuse for a court your father gave up for your mother's sake? No, it is Fairy Falls to which I refer."

Dread blossomed in my chest. "I thought he wasn't interested in our town."

Incredulity seeped into her expression. "Blair, your town represents the power Clearwater lost when the hunters cast him out. There, he was unmasked, and there, the fairies defied him and returned. Make no mistake, he plans to make the people of Fairy Falls pay for everything they cost him."

My mouth went dry, my heartbeat erratic. "It used to be your home, too. Your other daughter is still there."

"Blythe is beyond help," she said, "but I believe I can convince Rebecca to see things my way."

No. She won't. I'll get her out of here first.

Somehow. I didn't even know whereabouts in this vast house Rebecca was imprisoned, and despite Mrs Dailey's claims, I knew better than to believe her mother had let her roam free. No, she'd be in a cage just like me, even if it didn't have bars.

"I don't think you will." How to get out? She'd taken my wand, my wings were numb, and I assumed my fairy magic was beyond reach too. Maybe it'd return in time, but I might not have much of that left before Clearwater came back for me.

"I disagree." She turned her back and walked away.

As she left the room, I pushed forward in my seat, trying to beat my wings. A faint sensation returned but not enough.

The door closed behind Mrs Dailey, leaving me trapped. Again.

It took the better part of a day for sensation to return to my wings, and even then, I couldn't do much more than hover. I held the wall for balance as I did so, halting when the door nudged inward and a witch I didn't recognise put a tray of food on the floor. She withdrew just as quickly while I went to investigate. I couldn't tell if the contents of the plate were poisoned, like the net had been, but I wouldn't be taking any chances. Putting the plate down, I eyed the door, realising I hadn't heard a lock click. Wait a moment.

Experimentally, I moved to the door and pushed with one hand. The door swung outward, and a wide entrance hall greeted me on the other side, subtly different than during my last visit. The countless doors remained, as did the large plants placed at intervals, but there was no sign of the stair-case that usually dominated the lobby. Nor the front door. *That's inconvenient.*

With one hand on the wall for balance, I moved through the entrance hall to the next door along. As an experiment, I reached for the door handle and found none. It was a trick door with nothing but brick beneath.

"You can't get out." The witch who'd brought me the tray peered out from behind a plant pot. "There's no escape, not as long as *she's* here."

"You're a prisoner too?" I turned my back on the fake door. "You don't need to let her keep you trapped in your own home."

"Are you making a nuisance of yourself again, Blair?" Mrs Dailey walked into view as if she'd been watching from a distance the whole time, waiting for me to make an escape attempt. She probably had. "She's right, you know. The house is mine, and so is its magic."

Translation: there was no way out. Not for me or for Rebecca. I was well and truly stuck.

———

Knowing I was trapped didn't stop me from trying to find a gap in the bizarre magic of the house, but every attempt brought me to a dead end. Undeniably, the Knotgrass Coven's home was a marked improvement on the Lancashire Prison for Paranormals—I could see daylight, for a start, through the windows that moved out of reach whenever I drew close to them—and I had space enough to wander around. Even if there was nowhere to go.

By the following morning, my wings were functioning normally, and the effects of the net had worn off. I'd also paced every inch of the entrance hall, testing doors that led nowhere and windows that turned out to be mirrors in disguise. Even the ceilings eluded me when I flew upward in the hopes of finding the upper floor. This place was a giant maze designed to trap anyone that Mrs Dailey caught in her web, and I always ended up back in the same place as before.

"This is ridiculous." I talked to my own reflection in one of the mirrors lining the entrance hall out of the lack of any other options. "There's got to be a way to unravel the spell. The magic isn't even hers."

My fairy magic had begun to return along with the use of my wings, and sparks arose when I snapped my fingers, but I couldn't think of a single spell that might enable me to escape a magical trap like this one. I could unravel an illusion if a fairy had created it, but this was a witch's spell, not a fairy's. Frustrated, I snapped my fingers and conjured up a few sparks.

Wait. Could I use glamour?

I snapped my fingers experimentally, and my body vanished. Unfortunately, being able to turn invisible didn't matter if I couldn't get *out*. I might have tried disguising myself as one of the witches Mrs Dailey had working for her, but they weren't allowed out either.

Unless…

Picturing Rebecca's face in my mind's eye, I snapped my fingers and felt the illusion settle into place. Heart racing, I lifted my gaze to the mirror… which reflected Rebecca's face at me. I gave a double-take despite the fact that I *knew* it was my own face that lay beneath.

The mirror reflected the lie. Could I fool the house too? It was worth a shot. Reaching for one of the fake doors, I found the handle as unresponsive as ever. Maybe not, then.

I paced down the hall to the next mirror and then halted, frowning at my reflection. The mirror showed an elegant staircase behind me that definitely hadn't been there before but that *should* be here based on my past visit.

I spun around and choked on a gasp. The staircase had appeared as if out of nowhere… which wasn't inaccurate. I approached warily and placed a foot on the lowest step. Then the other foot. I began to climb, one step at a time, hardly daring to breathe.

When I heard footsteps above, I jumped violently. My wings beat on instinct, saving me from falling, but the staircase vanished beneath my feet, and so did the floor at the top.

"No," I hissed. "No. Come back."

I flew lower, my gaze fixed on the spot where the stairs were supposed to be, but they didn't reappear. Neither did the person whose footsteps I'd heard, but if the house was designed to react to anyone who set foot inside, my wings might have tipped it off that I wasn't Rebecca after all.

If I'd fooled the house once, I could do so again.

My feet touched down on the entrance hall carpet as I considered my next move. Evidently, the house could still sense me if I was invisible, but it didn't *know* me. I assumed Mrs Dailey had warped its magic to respond differently to herself and Rebecca than to anyone else, though Rebecca was just as much of a prisoner as I was. That left one other option if I wanted to get out.

I drew in a breath, called my fairy magic, and imagined Mrs Dailey's face in place of my own. In the nearest mirror, I watched the transformation take hold, and it was weird as hell to see Mrs Dailey's imperious face reflecting my own scared expression at me.

At once, the rooms around me began to warp and change. The entrance hall shrank, fake doors popping out of existence. I held my breath and waited tensely until the warping stopped.

As the house stilled, a single pair of doors remained at the very front of the entrance hall. *That's the way in. Or out.* Was it really that simple? I hardly dared to breathe as I paced towards the exit, making sure my feet touched the ground with every step despite my desire to take flight. Then I broke into a run, catching the door handles in both hands. They were reassuringly solid in my grip as I tugged them open.

"Stop right there, Blair Wilkes!" Mrs Dailey's voice rang out behind me.

The door handle vanished, but I was already launching myself forward and into flight. I reached the other side in the same instant that the doors disappeared.

I reeled on the spot, staring up at a blank wall. I was stranded on the outside instead of the inside. But where was Rebecca?

A rustling noise behind me prompted me to turn around. I stood at the top of a set of stone stairs above a garden that looked much less welcoming than the last time I'd been here. The hedges had become tangled masses blocking every way out, and judging from the way their branches reached for me, they sensed an intruder.

My wings beat, carrying me upward, as Mrs Dailey opened the door with a snarl. Flashes of light zipped past as I flew, narrowly dodging her spells. *Dammit, how do I get Rebecca out of there?* The house was a blank slate without another door or window to be seen.

As another jet of light skimmed the edge of my face, I

crashed headlong into someone in midair. The world flipped upside down.

The person I'd hit yelled, "You clumsy oaf!"

Of all the people to show up to my rescue... well, Blythe wasn't *quite* at the bottom of the list, given that her sister was held captive here, but still. I flipped the right way up, eyeing her sheepishly. "Blythe. Ow. Sorry."

"Where's my sister?" She leaned forward on the broomstick she rode, peering down at the open front door to the house.

"She's upstairs somewhere." I hovered on the spot. "The house wouldn't let me up there. Your mother warped its magic so that she's the only person who can go anywhere except the entrance hall, but I managed to use fairy magic to trick the house into letting me out."

"Then go back and rescue her!" She swore when another spell narrowly missed both of us. "Unless—my mother didn't wipe her memories, did she?"

"No." Guilt twisted inside me. I had to get her out of there somehow. "She thinks she can win Rebecca over without needing to use her powers."

She gave a short laugh. "Well, that's interesting, but she won't wait forever. Not when she finds out Clearwater has taken control of Fairy Falls instead of her."

"He *what?*"

Blythe forced another laugh. "Yeah. What did you expect after my sister was taken? It was only a matter of time before he found a gap."

No. It can't be.

Clearwater hadn't come after me yet... because he'd been too busy taking control of Fairy Falls instead.

14

I was still staring at Blythe when a rustling noise arose from the ground below. I looked down at the house, which was as starkly different on the outside as it was on the inside. The walls were smooth, windowless, and made of what appeared to be the kind of stone one associated with medieval castles. Mrs Dailey had turned the house and garden into a fortress. The source of the rustling was the hedges, which were rising higher to encompass the fences surrounding the house.

Blythe flew lower and swore under her breath. "She's back in the house. Why's she running away?"

"Maybe she's terrified of me." I peered down, seeing that the thorny hedges had crept right up the stone steps that led to the front door. Had she given up on me that easily? Or was she afraid we'd brought backup with us?

Blythe gave me an accusing stare. "What did you do to her?"

"Literally nothing." Did she seriously think I'd scared Mrs Dailey into running away? "She might be afraid that you brought half the town with you. Is it just you?"

"Yes," she said shortly. "I told you, Clearwater has Fairy Falls. Nobody can leave."

"That's impossible." It wasn't, not when Rebecca and her sceptre were here and not at Fairy Falls. But how could the defences have fallen that easily? Whatever had happened to the security team? "What about the fairies?"

"Not them," she replied. "I don't know where they went, but evidently, they didn't want to help the rest of us escape."

The fairies escaped. "Clearwater wants them dead, Blythe. They didn't have a choice."

The rustling noise ceased. Thorned hedges completely covered the grounds, while the house was a block of solid stone. I might have escaped by the skin of my teeth, but we'd have no chance of sneaking back inside to liberate Rebecca without help.

"Where are you going?" Blythe demanded as I began to fly away. "We can't leave my sister in there."

"Clearwater has Fairy Falls," I said over my shoulder. "Your mother wants your sister alive. Clearwater doesn't want the same for my friends."

"She sacrificed herself for you!" she exploded. "I can't believe this."

"I know." She didn't have to rub salt in the wound. "I know, but I can't get through those defences. Not alone. We need someone else's help."

We needed the fairies. My magic had temporarily fooled the house, but Mrs Dailey must have decided it wasn't worth keeping me under her watch. After all, she'd been saving me for Clearwater, and she must know my first stop after escaping would be Fairy Falls.

No matter whether I stayed or left, I'd already lost.

I picked up speed, the wind carrying my wings onward. Behind me, Blythe yelped, her broomstick caught in a tail-spin in the wake of my wings.

"Are you even capable of *not* being a disaster?" she bellowed at me.

I opened my mouth to reply and then yelped when the wind blew me off-course too. "It's not me!"

Air gusted towards both of us, revealing someone else flying at speed. Another fairy. Tensing, I lifted my hand to snap my fingers. Then I recognised him.

"Buck?" I lowered my hand, relieved to see a familiar face. "You're okay. Does that mean—Clearwater—?"

"Oh, he has Fairy Falls," Buck said grimly. "I saw Blythe leave town and wondered if she'd come to get you out."

"You were following me?" Blythe's eyes narrowed. "I guess it's okay if you're one of our fairies and not Clearwater's."

Our fairies? That was probably the closest she'd get to acknowledging that the fairies lived in Fairy Falls and weren't just there temporarily, but she could still have been a little nicer.

"Where are the others?" I asked. "Like Erin? *Nathan?*" Oh, god. Clearwater would never have left them alone, especially after their role in my escape from prison.

"Relax. They're safely in hiding." He turned around in midair. "I'll lead the way, but make sure nobody is following you."

"We're the only people here."

Yet I kept glancing over my shoulder as we flew over the countryside, half expecting Mrs Dailey to change her mind and follow. She seemed to have resigned herself to staying in hiding instead; that or she wanted to keep Rebecca at her side badly enough that losing me didn't matter.

Soon, we reached the lake near Fairy Falls, where Buck held out a hand to warn us to stop.

"We can't be seen," he told me. "Use glamour."

"Erm, what about Blythe?" Would she mind me using

glamour on her? I gave her a questioning look, but she returned it with a glare.

"Don't use your fairy magic on me." She pulled out her wand and cast an unseen spell on herself. Not as effective as glamour, but I figured it would be enough to stop anyone from noticing her approach.

I snapped my fingers to glamour myself invisible and made for the expanse of forest covering the northern edge of the lake, following the trail of faint sparks Buck had left in his wake to show me the way.

"This isn't inside Fairy Falls," I whispered, hoping he could hear me. "Where are we going?"

"Of course they aren't hiding *inside* Fairy Falls." Blythe's biting tone came out of the air next to me. "Honestly."

Yeah, but this is still close enough for Clearwater to find them.

As we neared the ground, I glimpsed a trail of sparks leading into the forest. I followed the trail and startled when a path appeared out of nowhere. Glamour shimmered at its edges. Had the fairies simply moved the entrance to their realm to another part of the woods?

"Is this enough to fool him?" I whispered. "Clearwater?"

"So far," Buck's voice answered. "It's this way."

"What am I supposed to be looking at?" Blythe dismounted her broomstick, looking around at the forest. "I don't know where your hiding place is."

"Follow our voices," I told her. "Buck, are you *sure* Clearwater doesn't know?"

"He might have a lot of allies, but he can't be in ten places at once." Buck's voice faded as he ascended the path.

I flew in behind him to avoid losing sight of the way in. A familiar clearing appeared before me, containing cottages surrounded by bright flowers. Buck turned visible again, and I snapped my fingers to undo my glamour.

As I did so, Sky came bolting towards me and slammed into my legs. "Miaow!"

"Hello to you too." I petted him, letting him wrap himself around my ankles, and saw one of the cottage doors open. "Dad?"

Once Sky had released me, my dad came over and swept me into a hug. "Blair. I was so worried about you."

"Same here." I hugged him back. "Where's everyone else? My foster parents? Nathan?"

"They're safe. Don't worry," he replied. "As soon as Clearwater moved in, we evacuated anyone who he was likely to target."

That meant my parents, my coworkers, my friends. "Ah, is Conor okay?"

His expression shadowed. "I don't know. He was still under the spell the Head Witch put on him when Clearwater's people showed up, so we weren't able to bring him to safety."

"Clearwater was there?"

"No, but the hunters had the town surrounded," he replied. "They set up more of those explosive spells at the borders. Trying to take out the defences while Rebecca was gone, I assume. The next thing we knew, Clearwater's people were marching into the town."

"I thought I was the one he wanted," I said. "Why didn't he follow Mrs Dailey?"

"He must have assumed she'd keep an eye on you while he drew Fairy Falls under his command." Bleakness coloured his tone. "This was always his aim, and if he finds the way into the forest... you weren't followed, were you?"

"No," Buck answered. "I checked. It's just us and Blair's friend."

I blinked in confusion before I remembered Blythe. She stood a short distance away, having removed her unseen spell, but the glower on her face indicated that she hadn't forgotten her sister's plight.

My dad looked between us. "You didn't get the Head Witch out?"

I dropped my gaze. "No. The instant I was outside, Mrs Dailey fortified the entire house against entry and set the hedges to attack anyone who went near the garden."

"That's no excuse for *abandoning* her," Blythe said pointedly.

"I'm not abandoning her." I looked pleadingly at my dad. "I just thought she was safer than the rest of us, at least for the time being. Is Clearwater inside Fairy Falls right this instant?"

"Clearwater isn't here," Dad said. "He'll be in the fairy realm, amassing his army."

My throat went dry. "To bring here? Or to attack your family?"

"Both, in all likelihood," he replied. "If he believes he can convince me to show him the way in."

"Does he think you'll cave in that easily?" If he still had Conor, though… *dammit*. "Have you spoken to your sister since he took over Fairy Falls?"

"I've sent messengers, but I don't dare go there myself in case Clearwater figures out a way to follow," he explained. "I fear it'll take a more direct threat for her to come to fight him in person."

"But does she know he has the Seeing Stone?" If he *did* find his way into her home, the Seeing Stone would enable him to bring her entire army under his own control. The sceptre might have been the biggest danger to the people of Fairy Falls, but to the fairies themselves, it was undoubtedly the Seeing Stone that would be the deciding factor in any war between them.

"Yes, which is partly why she hasn't come out to engage

with him directly," Dad said. "I managed to convey that in my messages, but it's hard to devise a plan without meeting face-to-face."

"I wish I had one too." I saw Blythe trying to get my attention, but she must have known it was unreasonable for me to try to convince the fairies to come to Rebecca's rescue when their own home was effectively under siege. "I wish Clearwater and Mrs Dailey *had* been at odds. That would have made things easier."

"Blair," Blythe hissed in my ear. "Your boyfriend's here."

Nathan. I swivelled on the spot, relief sweeping through me when I saw Nathan and Erin making their way up the path towards me.

"Nathan." I ran over and hugged him. "I'm glad you're okay."

"Same here." He briefly stroked my hair. "Is Rebecca not with you?"

"No. Mrs Dailey has her locked up."

We'd drawn more attention. Some of the fairies were emerging from the cottages in the clearing, while others climbed the path from the forest.

"Where have you been hiding out?" I asked. "Is half the town here?"

"No, but we tried to get everyone out who might be unduly targeted by Clearwater." Nathan took my hand and squeezed. "Your father helped us set up some safe houses. Your foster parents are in one of them. Alissa's been keeping them entertained."

"I owe her one." My shoulders slumped. "Sorry I got captured again. If not for me, Rebecca wouldn't have been taken, and the town wouldn't have fallen under Clearwater's control."

"Don't blame yourself, Blair," Nathan said firmly. "This

isn't your fault. Clearwater was waiting for an opening, and so was Mrs Dailey. It's hard to fight on two fronts at once."

"Don't I know it." I drew in a breath. "Is the town's entire security team obeying Clearwater now?"

"I haven't a clue." His expression shadowed. "Some of them might be resisting him, while others have escaped. Unfortunately, the more people we take in, the more likely it is that he'll realise where our hiding place is at some point."

"He can't get in," said my dad. "Not without following one of us."

"Until he hits one of you with that Seeing Stone," Blythe added helpfully.

Yeah, and Conor's out there too. I was sure my dad was worried about him, but he'd had to stay hidden for the sake of the others. Not to mention his sister. Like all of us, he wanted to protect too many people.

At Blythe's words, some of the other fairies exchanged worried mutters.

I cleared my throat. "Blythe, did you have a plan for liberating Fairy Falls from Clearwater's control? I'm sure if you did, the others would be willing to help you get Rebecca out of your mother's clutches."

"She's my *sister,*" Blythe said. "I want to get Rebecca away from there first, or else I won't help you fight Clearwater." She looked defiantly at everyone in the clearing, but nobody responded to her jab.

I felt another twinge of guilt on Rebecca's behalf, but what if Clearwater was hoping we'd mount a rescue mission so he could strike while we were out of hiding? That might well have been one of the reasons he'd timed his takeover to coincide with Rebecca's capture. Besides, if we *did* manage to subdue Mrs Dailey, it wasn't as if we could guarantee she'd stay contained. Not with the LPFP still under the control of the enemy.

I dragged my gaze from Blythe and realised everyone was looking at *me* instead, including my dad.

"What do you think we should do, Blair?" he asked.

"You want me to decide?" Heat rushed to my face, and my thoughts scrambled. "I don't know. I mean, if Clearwater is in the fairy realm, it's not like we can reach him from here."

"Technically, we can." Blythe spoke up. "If you haven't forgotten the portal."

The portal. A portal directly into Clearwater's home.

"That's *here?*" I looked to my dad, alarmed. "Shouldn't you have… I don't know, left it somewhere else?"

"It's defunct," he reminded me while the other fairies murmured among themselves. "The portal's safer with us, though if you don't mind me saying, I think it's unsafe for *any* of us to set foot in Clearwater's home."

"No kidding." I shook my head at Blythe. "I think we should leave the portal alone. Unless we can use it to lure him into a trap?"

"I doubt he'd fall for it," Dad commented. "The idea does have merit, though. I wonder what my sister would think."

"That's only half a plan," Blythe said. "What kind of trap would hold him?"

She'd made a good point, but it would have been nice if she didn't insist on shooting down all my ideas in front of my audience. "What's *your* plan, then?"

"Get my sister out of my mother's clutches," she replied. "Then she can use the sceptre to put up Fairy Falls's defences again."

"You don't think Clearwater would come back before then?" I queried. "Besides, I told you, that house is fortified, and everyone in there is as trapped as I was."

"What?" Her attention sharpened. "You didn't say there were other people in there. Who?"

"Witches," I said. "Members of the Knotgrass Coven,

maybe. I don't know. They wouldn't talk to me much, but they weren't there of their own free will."

Blythe swore. "Of course she would have ensnared anyone who came after the house after Arabella Knotgrass died."

Another thought hit me. "Wait—where's Madame Grey?"

"In her office. Where else?"

My heart missed a beat. "She's getting on with her job while the town is under control of a mad fairy?"

"Obviously," she said. "She doesn't run away when things get tough, unlike some people."

"Speak for yourself."

Madame Grey. Clearwater hadn't harmed her, had he? She'd played a role in his downfall as well, but it sounded as if Clearwater's attention was more fixed on the fairies than on the witches.

"She's in danger. So is anyone who supports her."

"Not Aveline," said Blythe. "She's gone."

"Aveline left town?" So much for her coming back in time to help Rebecca. Unless… "She hasn't gone to set Rebecca free, has she?"

"I doubt it," said Blythe. "I didn't see her, so I'm guessing she's gone into hiding. She's useless without a sceptre."

"What about the rest of the Knotgrass Coven?" Evidently, Mrs Dailey had expected an attack from somewhere, given the fortified state of the house when we'd escaped. "The ones who aren't held prisoner, I mean."

"I haven't a clue." She eyed the fairies, who were whispering among themselves again. "If you ask me, fairies have more of a chance of getting into that house. You managed to trick it into letting you out, didn't you?"

"Yeah, but…" But which other fairies would volunteer to put their own lives at risk for Rebecca's sake when they were already in mortal danger? I couldn't ask that of them. "As long as Clearwater's around, they can't leave the forest. You know that."

"Clearwater isn't here," she argued. "This is our chance. We can't waste it."

Exasperated, I turned to Nathan, who was conversing quietly with his sister. Erin looked as if she wanted to punch Blythe in the face, which was fair.

"Any ideas?" I asked them. "Where are Clearwater's hunter allies in all this? Has he left them behind?"

"He brought some with him," Nathan said, "but the majority are still at the prison, I think. His resources are split. That might work against him."

"Yeah. He can't use glamour on everyone at once." Same with the Seeing Stone, despite its abilities. I was immune to those.

"Miaow."

At first, I thought the noise had come from Sky, who'd curled up near my feet, but then I spied another cat across the clearing who looked almost identical to my familiar except for the lack of a white paw.

"Bronze." Dad strode to meet the cat. "Did you bring news from Lady Eventide?"

"Miaow." The little cat stuck out his tongue, to which was affixed a piece of paper.

When my dad retrieved the paper, Blythe made a soft noise of disbelief. "What's this?"

"It's news from a fairy queen," I told her. "If you're that bothered by us not immediately storming the Knotgrass Coven's house, why not go back there yourself?"

"You know why," she shot back at me.

Next to me, Dad straightened upright. "My sister wishes to speak to me."

"What?" I shook my head. "No way. That'll involve going out of the forest."

"Not necessarily," he said. "Clearwater isn't watching the northern shore of the lake."

"We'd still expose ourselves." Given the way Blythe was glaring at me, she might well dive into the lake to drag me straight back out again if I tried to follow my dad into the Eventide Court. "Besides, if she's not going to come and help us, it's not worth the risk."

"I'll go alone, then," Dad said. "I need to talk to her face-to-face."

"No way," I argued. "It's too risky. I know Clearwater isn't here, but—"

"Maybe your fairy sister will agree with your plan to lure him into a trap," Blythe interjected. "She might want in on it."

"She can't read our minds, Blythe." Unlike Blythe herself, for all the use that was at the moment. "Look, we can send her a letter instead, can't we, Dad?"

"Yes, if I knew what to say." He looked around the clearing, distracted. "My sister's letter implied that she stood a better chance of beating Clearwater in her own realm than here, but I don't know if she means she *wants* him to attack the Eventide Court."

"Why would she want that?"

"No idea." He sighed. "Blair, I should go and talk to her and ask for more details. She might be interested to know we have the portal too."

"If she wants the portal, she can have it," Blythe cut in. "In fact, would *that* be enough to convince her to come to our aid?"

"What, as a trade?" The portal might have belonged to the witches, but a fairy had played a part in its creation. And who knew, maybe Lady Eventide *would* want to get her hands on it. "Dad?"

"You're right." His expression cleared. "I never thought of that, but the portal is *very* valuable to the fairies."

"It also belongs to the Knotgrass Coven," Blythe added, which set off a chorus of disgruntled mutters among the fairies. "They might kick up a fuss."

"Blythe, you're the one who stole it from them in the first place." I gave her an eye roll. "I don't know that we need to bring a potential route into Clearwater's realm into your sister's home, though, Dad."

"Clearwater won't expect us to use it." A thoughtful expression came over his face. "Instead of waiting for Clearwater to attack, she'll be able to strike first. Get the upper hand."

"Hell of a risk," I murmured. "If Clearwater has a bigger army than hers."

"He doesn't." My dad turned to the other fairies. "Can someone bring me the portal?"

Several fairies ran off to fulfill his request, while I wondered if it would really be as simple as setting one fairy army on another and letting them finish each other off. No, my dad would never want his sister to fight Clearwater alone. And besides, Clearwater could still easily get into *this* realm whenever he wanted to.

Like it or not, though, while Lady Eventide might have been our only hope of challenging Clearwater's fairy army, handing the portal over to her might bring its own set of problems. Still, what choice did we have? Fairy Falls was under siege, my allies were on the run, and Rebecca was held hostage in a magical house under the control of someone whose own ambitions were unmatched by those of anyone but Clearwater himself.

Realisation settled in. I was going to have to go into the fairy realm again, and this time, I'd better hope I didn't fail at convincing Lady Eventide to help.

The lives of everyone in Fairy Falls might depend upon it.

15

This time, when my dad and I plunged into the lake, I managed not to let go of his hand. We surfaced, soaking wet, to the alarming sight of a thousand or more armoured fairies gathered on the bank.

"Whoa." I released my dad's hand and flew upward, my wings scattering droplets of water. "What's going on here?"

Countless fairies occupied the entire strip of land in front of the castle. They stood in formation, armed with spears and swords, dressed in glittering armour. It looked, in short, as if someone was expecting an attack.

"They're preparing to defend their home," Dad replied, scanning the shore. "Ah, there she is."

He flew towards one of the formations, where Lady Eventide was shouting orders in a lilting language I didn't understand. Like the others, she was dressed in gold armour, resplendent even on the brink of battle.

"Braden," she said, catching sight of us. "I wondered if you'd come. You didn't bring Clearwater with you, did you?"

"No," I answered, then flushed when she looked directly at me. "I think he's still in his own realm."

She gave a tinkling laugh. "Lost control of his armies already, has he?"

"I don't think so." I looked to my dad questioningly. "He can't have, can he?"

"No, but I doubt he's having as easy a time commanding his forces as he did previously," he said. "Don't forget he was absent for years, living in the human world. I've seen for myself that not everyone is willing to accept that."

A pang hit my heart, knowing he was talking about his own family.

"You're different," I whispered to him. "He was gaining power in the human world, and you were only trying to keep me and my mother safe."

"Clearwater might live to regret his choices," said Lady Eventide, "but I'm curious as to why you both came here again. Do you wish to join my army?"

"We..." I faltered, seeing my dad waiting for me to speak first. "We have something that we think you want."

"Oh?" She arched one brow. "What is it, pray tell?"

"A portal directly to Clearwater's home."

"That *is* valuable." Her eyes gleamed with interest. "Where is it?"

"At home." We'd decided against bringing it with us in case we did get ambushed on our way out of the forest, though the fairies would have the portal ready for us when we got back. "But we can give you the portal if you help us fight Clearwater."

With every word I spoke, I was conscious of every fairy in the army watching me, a half-human outsider, negotiating with their queen.

"You would offer me a direct route through which to attack our enemy without passing through the human realm." A smile flickered on her lips. "Tempting."

"You think you can beat him?" I spoke carefully, not

wanting to offend her. "Ah, did my dad tell you about his new weapon?"

Dad cleared his throat. "Blair wants to know what you plan to do about the Seeing Stone. Its magic enables him to control any fairy who comes near him."

"A human-made artefact, is it?" she queried.

"No, the fairies made it." I gave my dad a questioning look. "Didn't they?"

"I believe the fairies know it by a different name," he said. "It's one of the artefacts claimed by the covens, at any rate." He then spoke a word I didn't understand, but that caused his sister's eyes to widen.

"The thieving humans do have a habit of taking our artefacts," she said. "Would you trade *that* to me?"

Uh oh. It was news to me that the Seeing Stone *was* the fairies' creation, but I could only imagine the level of havoc it'd wreak if anyone who got their hands on it was able to control the minds of every other fairy within reach.

"No," my dad said, his tone quiet but firm. "It's not ours to trade, and it's currently in Clearwater's possession besides."

"Isn't the portal enough?" I asked without thinking, flushing bright red when my words drew everyone's attention back to me. "Ah, sorry, but we don't have much time. Clearwater has taken over Fairy Falls altogether and driven all the fairies into hiding, and one of his allies has captured a friend of mine too."

"So I see." She studied me, her green eyes bright beneath her golden helmet. "What would you ask of me, Blair Wilkes?"

"For your help." It didn't matter if she didn't leave her own realm, not if we could bring Clearwater here. But doubt remained lodged in my chest, knowing the Seeing Stone might topple even her formidable army. "In exchange for the portal."

Lady Eventide pursed her lips. "I cannot bring my army to your realm, Blair Wilkes. You'll have to bring him to me."

"That, we can do," Dad said. "Would you prefer to mount an ambush yourself, or would you like us to attempt to lure Clearwater out alone?"

Alone. Would that work? Clearwater certainly wouldn't expect Lady Eventide to attack first, but the notion of trying to lure an immortal fairy into a trap struck me as something that might backfire spectacularly.

Lady Eventide gave a laugh. "I'd certainly like to see Clearwater's face if you managed to trick him."

"We don't need to bring him through the portal directly, though," I said, thinking back to my arrival here. "We can use the lake, and that way, he wouldn't have his army with him."

"Not a bad idea," Dad said, "but in order to use the lake as a portal, one of us would have to risk getting close enough to Clearwater to fall within range of his weapons. We'd also have to risk his allies following us through."

That's true. "We'll see if Clearwater takes the bait first, but if he does come here, I'll need a guarantee that he won't immediately escape."

"Oh, he won't," said Lady Eventide with a vicious smile. "Let's see if those weapons of his can stand against mine."

Can she beat the sceptre and *the Seeing Stone, though?* Maybe she could, maybe not, but the rest of us sure as hell couldn't. We'd have to hope her confidence wasn't misplaced.

"I'll bring you the portal as soon as I can," Dad told her. "Clearwater is watching my people, so we have to be careful. In the meantime, I'd be ready for his arrival here."

Her smile widened. "I look forward to it."

Worries bubbled up inside me as my dad and I turned back to the lake. I didn't quite dare ask the obvious question until we'd plunged below the surface and emerged back outside Fairy Falls.

"Can she do it?" I snapped my fingers to glamour myself unseen in case anyone was watching from across the lake. "Can she beat him?"

"Without a doubt," he replied. "If we were to lure him there alone, he'd likely find himself in trouble."

"Only if we get that Seeing Stone off him."

"There you are," said a voice.

I jumped. I'd failed to spot Blythe waiting expectantly on the shore, a broomstick at her side.

"Have you been standing there all this time?" The forest shielded her from most angles, but anyone who looked across the lake would spot her in an instant. "How long have we been gone?"

"Long enough," she replied. "Clearwater knows you're back. He has people patrolling the border."

My heart lurched. "Where?"

She pointed at the mass of trees behind her. "They're searching the forest. I couldn't find my way back without drawing their attention."

"You shouldn't have left in the first place," I told her. "If Clearwater's people saw you..."

"They aren't looking for me." She lifted her chin in defiance. "I'm beneath their notice."

"Clearwater isn't here, right?" Dad asked warily. "Where's the portal?"

"Where I left it," she replied. "Did your plan work? Did you make a deal with the fairies?"

"Yes, but it depends on us taking Clearwater to them..." I trailed off as a muffled blast echoed from somewhere on the other side of the forest. "What was that?"

Were Mrs Dailey's dimwitted allies up to their old tricks again? They didn't need to blow open the border to get inside the town, but if they'd found my allies...

As I prepared to take flight, a loud explosion of fireworks

across the sky made me startle. "That hadn't been in Fairy Falls. What—?"

Blythe smiled enigmatically. "Just some of my allies sending a signal."

"You have *allies?*" More time must have passed than I'd thought, but it was better than finding Clearwater had found my friends' hiding place while we'd been gone. "What signal?"

"Don't sound so surprised." She crouched, picking up her broomstick. "I had to do something useful while you were gallivanting off. Let's go."

"Go where?" Wait. The fireworks had come from the same direction as the Knotgrass Coven's home. "If your allies are trying to rescue Rebecca, why aren't you with them?"

She sneered. "Why'd you think? I thought you were bringing help."

"You thought a bunch of fairies would agree to rescue a human they'd never met?" Honestly. "They aren't even coming to help Fairy Falls. And if Clearwater's people are at the border, they'll know the instant we leave."

"Not if we move fast." She mounted her broomstick. "Well?"

Dammit. If Blythe's supposed allies were attacking Mrs Dailey, Rebecca might end up caught in the crossfire no matter what.

My dad caught my arm. "I can stall them. Give you time to get Rebecca out of there and to our hideout. Clearwater hasn't found our hiding place in the forest yet."

"He might." It was just like Blythe to force my hand, but the sparks flying across the sky indicated her allies were putting up a fight of their own. "Who *is* that?"

"Aveline."

"Seriously?" If Aveline expected to single-handedly liberate Rebecca, she wasn't likely to have much luck, but the number of sparks flying across the sky indicated she wasn't alone. "Fine. I'm going, but, Dad, you can't hold off Clearwater's people alone. Do you want to come with me? It might be safer than here."

Dad didn't reply. He'd gone completely still, wings beating, his attention fixed on a spot north of the lake.

"Dad?"

He dragged his gaze away. "Conor's here. Clearwater must have brainwashed him again."

Conor. Oh, no. If we went out into the open, he'd see right through any spell that Blythe and I used to hide ourselves.

"We can fly around him." Blythe was already on her broomstick, hovering several inches off the ground. "I'm not going to let anyone stop me."

And she was off, a breeze stirring up in her wake. Shivering, I remembered my sopping-wet clothes. I grabbed my wand and cast a quick drying spell before taking flight too. My dad rose into the air next to me, glamouring himself unseen, but not before I saw his gaze travel to the other side of the forest, where a figure paced along the border. *Conor.*

"Dad, don't." I glamoured myself invisible too. "You know what happened the last time."

"I know." I heard him sigh, but he moved in to fly alongside me. "I just wish I could help him."

"We'll come back," I whispered to him. "And we'll set him free."

Somehow. Clearwater wasn't here in person, but it was only a matter of time before he lost his last shred of patience and came to enact revenge on everyone who'd defied him.

But Rebecca needed us too. We flew eastward over the lake, towards the fireworks signalling the way. Lights continued to flicker across the sky, and I could only hope that they were coming from our own side and not Mrs Dailey's.

Blythe stopped in midair, almost causing me to crash into her back, as a winged figure ascended in front of us. *Conor.*

"I can see you, Blair," he said in a monotone. "Come with me."

When he lunged, I darted upward, but not fast enough to avoid his hands grabbing my ankles. "Let go of me!"

Conor bared his teeth in a snarl. "Don't fight me, Blair."

"Clearwater is controlling you." I might as well have spoken to a brick wall. "Don't do this, Conor. You'll regret it."

Conor dragged me downward while I struggled to escape his hold. *How can he still be under Clearwater's control when the Seeing Stone isn't here?* Surely, it had a limit somewhere.

"Conor, resist him." I snapped my fingers. A curtain of glitter overlaid my vision as I conjured up the first image to come to mind: my cat, climbing up his arm.

As I'd hoped, Conor hissed in anger and let go of me. He grabbed for me again when he realised Sky wasn't actually here, but a blast of light came streaking at him from behind. He dodged, spinning to face his attacker. Blythe. She hadn't flown off and abandoned me, for a wonder.

"Leave him, Blair," she ordered. "He's a lost cause."

You want him to follow us to your sister? I swallowed the words as I noticed an odd flickering light playing across Conor's face. A similar light spun around my fingertips, remnants of the illusion I'd conjured. Wait, was Clearwater's spell a *glamour?* If the fairies had had a role in creating the Seeing Stone, it would certainly make sense. And I knew how to unravel regular glamour.

It was my last idea, so when Conor flew at me, I twisted out of reach, extending a hand towards the shimmering lines above his face.

The sensation was like grabbing a spiderweb. The instant I seized the spell, it slipped through my grasp, but sticky threads remained affixed to my hands. Conor stopped in midgrab, his mouth agape.

"Fight him!" I shouted, seizing the glamour with both hands. "Break his hold!"

Connor staggered as I gave a huge tug, yanking the glamour away from him like a heavy net. I staggered, too, unprepared for the weight of it. But the instant I released the threads, they dissipated in the air as if they'd never existed.

Shimmering light appeared at my shoulder as my dad lifted his own glamour. "Conor? Blair, what was that?"

"I tried to undo the spell." I stared at the other fairy. "Conor, did it work?"

Conor himself remained rooted to the spot as if in shock, the only movement from his beating wings until he lifted his head. "Blair?"

"You're back?" My dad studied his face then embraced his friend. "I'm glad. I thought Clearwater had completely brain-washed you."

Conor stiffened. "I'm sorry. I should never have gone to face him alone."

"I'm just glad you're okay," said Dad. "You're lucky."

"As are you." Conor eyed me. "Blair, you set me free. If there's anything I can do to repay you, please, let me know."

I hesitated. "Well, we were just on our way to rescue Rebecca from Mrs Dailey. She's claimed the Knotgrass Coven's house. Also, she hates fairies but doesn't have a clue how to fight us, so we hoped we could best her. If you'd like to help…"

Conor grinned, startling me into stopping my babbling. "Yes. I see. That Dailey woman deserves the wrath of our kin for what she did to us. I would be glad to help you."

He said yes? Unable to quite believe my luck, I flew to catch up with Blythe. We cleared the edge of the lake without running into any more of Clearwater's allies, though I knew it would only be a matter of time before he figured out what I'd done.

We have to stop Mrs Dailey first. When we had Rebecca out of her hands—I couldn't guarantee her safety in Fairy Falls, but the same could be said of anywhere else—we'd be free to focus all our attention on bringing down Clearwater.

We flew north, the three of us, closing in on the fireworks exploding across the sky. When we neared the Knotgrass Coven's house, I saw the source: several witches standing on the hillside with their wands in the air. The house remained locked in defensive mode, and every spell bounced off its hedges and walls, but the witches showed no signs of slowing down.

I slowed my pace and spoke to Dad and Conor. "The house is reinforced, but it can't detect fairies, I don't think. If we glamour ourselves, we might be able to get in."

"Through where?" Conor asked. "There isn't a door or window to be found."

True. The gates were barred and locked, and hedges grew across any possible entrance. Was it even possible to stealthily sneak into a place that well defended? Surely not, but I had to wonder what the witches who stood nearby had hoped to achieve.

Blythe was already flying down to meet them. I angled myself downward and was rewarded with several shrieks when I snapped my fingers to reveal myself to the witches. Only Aveline looked unsurprised to see me. She was grin-ning in amusement, her wand pointed at the Knotgrass Coven's home as she unleashed an endless streak of vibrant sparks.

"Is that actually helping?" I asked her. "You can't touch the house, can you?"

"No, but I can do my best to make it as unpleasant for its inhabitant as possible."

As the world's worst houseguest, she was well practised at driving people out of their minds inside their own homes, I supposed. Though the house didn't belong to Mrs Dailey. And neither did the Knotgrass Coven's magic.

"It won't work if she cast a soundproofing spell, though." I pointed out. "What did you plan to do, keep hitting the house until she gets annoyed enough to come out?"

"I'm sure you can think of a better way to lure our intruder out of hiding, Blair."

"Were you waiting for me to come and figure it out for you?" Annoyance flared inside me, and then an idea struck like a lightning bolt.

"You thought of something, didn't you?" Aveline gave me a knowing smirk. "I look forward to seeing it."

"Don't get too excited." I scanned the skies for my dad and saw him and Conor hovering a short distance away. Flying up to meet them, I asked, "Can you conjure up an illusion big enough to cover the whole house?"

"What kind of illusion?" asked Conor.

"Clearwater." I looked between my dad and his friend. "His army. I think *that* would lure her out of hiding, don't you?"

"She won't be fooled," said Conor. "Not if she looks up close."

"It doesn't matter," I replied. "We'd just need to get her outside. The witches will do the rest."

"I will," Blythe corrected, having followed me. "You'd better not screw this up."

"Thanks for the vote of confidence."

I flew down to tell the witches the plan first. Aveline scowled when I told her to stop throwing fireworks at the house, but she complied. Well, well. Maybe she had faith in me after all.

I returned to my dad and Conor, faced the house, and

lifted my right hand. In my mind's eye, I tried to picture Clearwater's army of fairies. I might not have known exactly what it looked like, but Lady Eventide's army had given me a fair idea, and I only needed to do a small part of the illusion myself.

While my dad and Conor conjured up a sweeping illusion of an army descending upon the house, I snapped my fingers, picturing Clearwater's face. I didn't need to try very hard, since his face was etched into my mind's eye as clearly as my own.

Time to see if it fools Mrs Dailey.

Head held high, I took flight over the garden. I looked upon the Knotgrass Coven's house with the enemy's face and waited for Mrs Dailey to emerge.

16

For a heartbeat, nothing happened. Then, the hedges withdrew a little, revealing an area near the front doors. *The doors.* Instinct urged me to grab them before they disappeared again, but if I wanted to do this right, I had to wait for her to open them from the inside.

Mrs Dailey's head appeared in a downstairs window, her eyes widening in surprise. "What are *you* doing here?"

I didn't reply, not trusting my voice not to give me away. Instead, I beckoned, indicating that I wanted to talk outside. She vanished from view, and I waited, heart in my throat, until the front door opened.

Mrs Dailey stepped outside. "This wasn't part of our arrangement, Clearwater," she said haughtily. "You said I could have the witches. What are you doing here?"

I remained silent, doing my best impression of the Inquisitor's glare.

"What is it?" she pressed. "What do you want?"

I spoke, my voice raspy. "Rebecca."

And with a snap of my fingers, I conjured up a swirl of glitter straight into her eyes. As she staggered, a dozen spells hit her head-on, sending her tumbling down the front steps. My dad and Conor closed in, seizing her by the arms and lifting her into the air.

"Now!" Aveline shrieked, but I didn't hear the rest of her order.

Blythe flew into me from behind, knocking me off balance, so intent upon flying through the open door that she hardly noticed the witches' spells narrowly missing her.

"Wait!" I flew behind Blythe, a spell sizzling past my ear, while Mrs Dailey shrieked obscenities from the sky. "Blythe, don't touch the ground. The house will react to you."

"I'm not an imbecile," she bellowed, gripping her broomstick as she steered her way into the entrance hall.

I followed, careful not to let my own feet touch the ground as I flew through the entrance hall, but there was still no sign of the staircase to the upper floor. I'd let my glamour slip, but Clearwater wasn't one of the people who had access to the house.

Trying to ignore the noise from outside, I pictured Mrs Dailey's face and snapped my fingers. The instant my feet touched the ground, the hall began to shift and change, and a staircase sprang up like a tree grown out of the floorboards.

"Rebecca!" I called out. "Come downstairs! It's me!"

Footsteps sounded, but they came from downstairs. One of the Knotgrass witches emerged from a room with her eyes wide as if she'd never seen daylight before. Upon seeing me, she recoiled. Oh, wait. I was still wearing Mrs Dailey's face.

"It's not her," I said. "I mean, I'm not her. I'm here to rescue you. Where's Rebecca?"

"Blair!" Rebecca herself appeared at the top of the stairs, eyeing me in shock. "It *is* you, isn't it?"

"Of course it is." I suppressed the impulse to fly upstairs in case the house hid the staircase again. "Is anyone else upstairs?"

"I don't think so." She ran, meeting me at the foot of the stairs, and threw herself at me with a sob. "I thought you'd gone."

"I'd never have left you here." Hearing Blythe scoff behind me, I gently pried Rebecca off me. "We'd better get out of here before the house realises we're escaping."

"Then can you put your real face back on?" Rebecca said. "I don't think my mother has ever hugged me in her life. Where is she?"

"On her way to prison if I have anything to do with it." Blythe reached for her sister's hand and helped her climb onto the back of her broomstick. "Let's go."

More witches emerged, blinking, from the rooms as the pair of us made for the door, where I dropped my glamour and took to the sky. Nearby, I saw that Aveline and her companions had Mrs Dailey surrounded, while Conor looked on in satisfaction.

Then the obvious hit me. "Where's the sceptre?"

Rebecca grimaced. "I think she locked it up. She was going to ask Clearwater to make it obey her and not me."

Oh boy. I looked to her sister, but Blythe didn't slow her flight. "I'm not going back in there."

"You don't mind leaving it behind?"

Rebecca shook her head. "No. It won't obey anyone else."

At least there was that, but we wouldn't be able to put the defensive spell around Fairy Falls without the sceptre. Given that Clearwater already had control of the town, it wouldn't necessarily make a difference to our chances anyway, and there was no way I would risk getting stuck in that house again. Blythe didn't seem to have any intention of turning back, either. *So be it.*

I beckoned to my dad and Conor, but only the former flew to catch up with me. Conor's attention remained riveted on the captive Mrs Dailey, his eyes narrowed in anger.

"Conor," Dad called to him. "Are you ready?"

He bared his teeth. "She deserves to pay for what she did. I would like to ensure she receives the justice she's brought upon herself."

"What about Clearwater?" I asked. "You can stay if you like, but I want to make sure he hasn't attacked Fairy Falls while we were gone."

Blythe was already flying onward at speed, and I hastened to catch up to her. "Blythe, what if Clearwater has found the fairies' hiding place? He was already searching the forest."

"We'll work something out," she said shortly without looking at me. "Anywhere's better than here."

"Blythe, seriously, we don't have the sceptre." I knew it was futile to argue, but if she wasn't careful, she'd fly her sister straight into another trap. "And he already has Fairy Falls."

"He doesn't have my mother." She sounded almost exhilarated. "I bet he thought of her as a backup plan, and without her, he'll have less chance of catching us. He can't be in three places at once."

I wasn't quite that optimistic, but she might have had a point about Clearwater splitting his attention in too many directions at once. "We still need an alternative. We don't want to fly into his clutches."

"She's right," my dad told her. "You remember how close Clearwater's followers were to the border, don't you?"

Blythe scowled. "If they're still around, I'll handle them."

Giving up on convincing her for now, I flew back to join my dad. Conor had reluctantly peeled away from the witches to join us. "Conor, do you remember anything from when Clearwater was controlling you? Did he happen to mention his plans?"

"He did, but I'm not sure if he told me anything we don't already know." His expression clouded. "He intended to make a claim on Fairy Falls while the Head Witch was captured, and I was supposed to assist in the diversion. Then he sent me to lead the hunt for the people who escaped to the forest."

"I'm glad our protections held up," Dad said. "And even gladder that Blair was able to undo the spell on you."

"I didn't know I'd be able to do that," I admitted. "Maybe it's because he can't use the Seeing Stone on me."

"He can't?" Conor's eyes widened. "If that's the case, perhaps you'll stand a chance at removing him from power."

"Oh, no," I said hastily. "I can't beat him alone. He still has the sceptre, but Dad convinced his sister to help us."

"He told me," said Conor. "However, I didn't have the impression Lady Eventide intended to come here herself."

"She wants us to lure Clearwater into her realm," I explained. "I'm the one he wants, so I guess I could try to bait him as long as he doesn't see through the ruse."

"Offering Lady Eventide the portal in exchange might end up being a mistake," he added, addressing my dad.

"I know," Dad said, "but it was all I could think of, and let's face it, the portal is likely to cause nothing but strife in the human world."

No kidding. It'd caused enough controversy among the witches when they'd discovered Arabella Knotgrass had been keeping a passage into the fairy realm in her home. After her death, there might have been a scramble for ownership if not for the fact that Blythe had already stolen the portal herself. Who knew, maybe it'd be safer in the fairy realm after all.

As we flew south, I glimpsed several other winged figures ahead of us, descending on the lake. *Please tell me that isn't Clearwater.*

Tension zipped up my spine, and I halted in midair. "Dad, is that him?"

"If it isn't, it's definitely his people," Dad replied grimly.

"I'd say he's either found our hiding place, or he knows we took down Mrs Dailey."

"Blythe, wait." I flew in behind her and Rebecca. "The fairies are there. They'll be watching the sky for us."

"We can't go in on the ground," she argued. "They're at the border too."

"Did you want to fly right into his army?" I cursed under my breath as she continued, evidently set on her own path without any care for the consequences.

As we drew nearer to Fairy Falls, the sound of fighting reached my ears. Snarls and roars echoed from the forest, while sparks flew into the air above the lake. Not just fairy magic was in play but witch magic too. Clearwater's forces had attacked Fairy Falls, but they hadn't found it undefended.

Werewolves swarmed north of the lake, while some of the fairies who'd gone into hiding had emerged to fight against Clearwater's allies. Conor and my dad flew in to join them, but I found my attention drawn to the sound of another commotion that had broken out somewhere near the university campus. When I flew closer, I glimpsed a group of people fleeing uphill, chased by...

"Is that a flying carpet?" Rebecca asked, echoing my own thoughts.

"Looks that way." Sitting on the carpet were what could only be students—accompanied, inexplicably, by Samuel the librarian. "I think they're kicking out the hunters."

In the lead of the fleeing group of hunters, I recognised Linda Graham, amongst others. Upon spotting me, she skidded to a halt, her mouth twisting in anger. "Stop fleeing! Fight back!"

Speak for yourself. It'd looked to me as if she was leading the escape, and no wonder. Alongside the carpet flew a pair of what I might have taken to be actual dragons if not for the telltale gleam of glamour surrounding their reptilian forms.

One of the dragons roared, and Linda Graham's brief moment of nerve vanished. She broke into a sprint again, while I spied Rosalyn and Ani among the students on the carpet, conducting the illusory dragons with mischievous giggles.

As the hunters ran for the northern border, none other than Madame Grey stepped out to meet them. Her face was taut with fury, and she seemed oblivious to the bloodthirsty roars from the werewolves in the forest not five metres away from her.

The group of fleeing hunters came to an instant stop, looking around for another escape route. And then one of them spotted Blythe's broomstick.

"Hey!" Grumpy pointed at the sky. "It's the Head Witch!"

"Get her!" Linda Graham directed the hunters to turn away from Madame Grey, but how she expected them to jump twenty feet into the air to grab the broomstick, I had no idea.

Sleepy made a valiant effort, only to trip and fall on his face instead. Dopey and Grumpy closed in behind, but Blythe ignored them and continued to fly. If I'd had to guess, she planned to take Rebecca and barricade herself in the house until the coast was clear, which wasn't the worst idea, assuming Clearwater himself didn't come to take back control of Fairy Falls himself.

"We'll get her," Grumpy announced, charging after Blythe and Rebecca. "C'mon."

Sleepy and Dopey gave chase, too, only to scatter when the flying carpet came soaring towards them.

"It's over," I told the hunters. "We beat your master. Mrs Dailey has surrendered to the witch council."

"No!" they chorused. "Impossible."

"Not at all." Blythe grinned in triumph from the back of her broomstick as she left us in the dust.

"It's the Head Witch!" Dopey exclaimed, as quick on the uptake as usual.

"What part of 'Mrs Dailey has surrendered' don't you understand?" I shook my head at them.

A flurry of sparks flew into the air near the border, prompting me to turn in that direction. Madame Grey had engaged the fleeing hunters in battle, and when I flew over to meet her, I saw some familiar faces emerging from the forest.

Alissa waved up at me. "Hey, Blair!"

"Alissa." I landed and hugged her. "Where—?"

"Your parents are okay. Don't worry," she said. "I'm going back to the hospital to help anyone who needs it, though it looks like we're winning this round."

"Don't speak too soon." I winced when a series of angry growling noises arose from the forest. The fairies had *really* underestimated the power of a wrathful werewolf pack who'd had their territory invaded. "Clearwater isn't here yet, but I can guarantee he will be when he realises the hunters are on the run. Did you plan this?"

"Me?" she echoed. "No, but I think we had five or six rebellions going on at the same time. Oh, there's your boyfriend."

My attention snapped towards the forest, from which Nathan and Erin had emerged to join the fray. Buck, too, flew in to fight on the side of our allies, his hands alight with vibrant fairy magic.

"Blair!" Nathan ran over to me. "You found Rebecca?"

"Yes, and we stopped Mrs Dailey. Aveline and others are restraining her as we speak." A flurry of sparks flew overhead, and I ducked. "Clearwater will be on his way here. We have to be ready."

"Blair!" Erin joined her brother. "Good, you didn't get captured this time. I was starting to think that cat of yours might need to break you out."

"Where is Sky?" I looked around, but the thick trees coupled with the general confusion of the fight made it hard to see if my cat might be hiding somewhere nearby.

"He went that way." She pointed vaguely at the woods. "He said it was important, I think. It's hard to understand when he only talks in meows."

"Erin!" Buck flew over to us, having momentarily abandoned the fleeing hunters. "Your family... they're over there. I think they want to talk to you."

Erin and Nathan both turned towards the border, stiffening when they saw who waited for them. Eric, Jay, and Mr Harker. *What are they doing here?*

"He wants to do this now? Really?" Erin began to march north, her face set. "Bring it on."

"Wait." Nathan strode in behind her, while I hastened to catch up in case Clearwater had sent Nathan's family here as a diversion. The three of them didn't look as if they'd come to join in the fight, though. They looked more like a group of lost hikers.

"Nathan." Mr Harker studied his two other children as they approached. "Erin."

"What's all this?" Erin demanded. "If you want to help the group of scumbags who tried to take over Fairy Falls, you're too late. They're already on the run."

"That's not why we're here," Eric said, with a touch of hesitation. "We're..."

"We're here to help," Mr Harker finished.

I goggled at them. So did Nathan.

Erin, however, laughed. "Yeah, right."

"It's true," Eric said defensively. "I helped you break Blair out of jail, remember?"

"You still stayed with him," she said. "With Clearwater."

"You needed people on the inside, didn't you?" He wore a defiant expression. "I can tell you there was an uprising in the jail not long after the breakout, which took all Clearwater's efforts to calm down. That's why he didn't catch up to you right away."

"You're welcome," added Jay. "That was my doing."

"Good for you." The heat had gone out of Erin's voice, though. "What made you change your mind?"

Mr Harker cleared his throat. "I talked to several of my colleagues among the hunters, those whose memories of the former Inquisitor weren't quite as hazy."

"I knew he couldn't have mind-controlled all of them." I didn't entirely trust the other Harker siblings, but I'd take all the allies I could get. "Where is Clearwater?"

"In the fairy realm, I assume," Eric said. "He left the hunters to pick up the pieces after the ruckus at the jail. I don't see many of them coming to help."

"He still has his fairy army," Erin observed. "Though we have one of our own, right, Blair?"

"Provisionally." I tensed when Nathan's family members all turned towards me. "And they aren't coming here."

"What do you want us to do?" The question came from Mr Harker, and he sounded serious, for a wonder. Eric and Jay also watched me expectantly, as if they genuinely wanted me to tell them what to do. Flustered, I looked to Nathan, who smiled encouragingly at me.

"Right. We need to get Clearwater over there." I pointed to the lake. "Preferably alone. There's an army waiting on the other side of the portal to my dad's realm, but we need to get him to drop that Seeing Stone. No fairy can go near it without being mind-controlled."

"That means you, Buck," Erin said. "Stay out of the line of fire."

Her fiancé scowled. "Fine. I'll see if your father needs any help with the portal, Blair."

"Is that where he is?" I'd lost sight of Conor, too, but the werewolves seemed to have sent Clearwater's fairies into retreat. "Clearwater didn't bring much of an army, did he?"

"I think those fairies are from this realm," Nathan said quietly. "Not from Clearwater's court."

"That would explain it." Clearwater's fairy army might well have been as reluctant to set foot in the human realm as Lady Eventide's was. It would certainly explain why we hadn't seen any signs of them yet, but ideally, we needed to pit his forces against hers, not against Fairy Falls. "I need to find my dad. Can you tell as many people as possible that we need help to lure Clearwater to the lake?"

Trusting Nathan and Erin to keep an eye on their siblings and father, I took flight over the forest. At the northern border, the escaped hunters cowered in front of Madame Grey and her fellow witches, while the flying carpet had landed nearby. Elsewhere, a few people were out in the streets of Fairy Falls, watching the skies warily as if anticipating an attack. I didn't see anyone at the southern boundary, but a dazzling light drew my gaze to the lake. My dad had emerged from the forest, carrying one end of a large mirror—or rather, portal. Conor held the other end, while Sky the cat padded at their side.

"Miaow!" Sky yowled when he saw me flying down to meet them.

"There you are." I stroked Sky, eyeing the shimmering surface of the portal. "Are you taking that to your sister?"

"Once we're sure it's functioning," Dad replied. "It needs to be tested to see if it works, but I doubt anyone in their right mind would volunteer to try it out."

"To do what?" My heart jolted. "To go into Clearwater's home and goad him into coming out?"

Could he hear us through the portal right now? I hoped not. My skin crawled as I looked at the shimmering surface, but all I saw was my own reflection, slightly blurred at the edges.

"Miaow." Sky jabbed a paw at the mirror.

"What?" I blinked uncomprehendingly. Then it hit me. "You want to volunteer?"

"Fairy cats aren't bound by the usual laws of requiring an invitation to visit another fairy's domain," my dad said thoughtfully. "If he were to go through alone, he might be able to lure Clearwater out. But the portal isn't functioning yet. It needs to be recharged after being rendered defunct for so long."

"What, like a battery?" I surveyed the mirror with less wariness than before. "How do we do that?"

"We'll need a surge of magic," Conor said. "I believe the falls will suffice."

"Right. The waterfall." My heartbeat kicked up erratically. "Once it opens, will Clearwater come out?"

"No. He doesn't need a portal to get here, remember?" Dad said. "He might not know what's happening over here yet, but if your cat shows up, he'll certainly take notice."

Then he'll fly straight into our trap. "We'll need to be ready to take the Seeing Stone away from him." To stop Clearwater from capturing Lady Eventide's army under his spell, we had to take away his advantage.

While Dad and Conor continued to carry the portal, I spied Nathan and his family approaching from the forest. Behind them walked a number of witches, werewolves, and even elves. They began gathering on the shores of the lake.

"What are they all doing here?" asked my dad.

"I told Nathan to bring everyone possible to the lake." I took in a breath. "If everyone's waiting for Clearwater when he shows up, we'll stand more of a chance at taking him by surprise."

"Then we won't delay." Conor hefted his end of the portal

into the air, and he and my dad carried it towards the path leading to the falls. Sky padded at my side, occasionally rubbing against my leg and demanding a stroke, while Dad and Conor manoeuvred the mirror downhill towards the Fairy Falls. The rippling curtains of water were unchanged, but the air felt charged as if with static electricity.

At the foot of the slope, the two of them adjusted their grips on the mirror and tilted it upward so that the spray from the falls caught on the glass. My breath caught when the water bounced straight off the surface as if repelled by an invisible force.

"More." Dad pushed the mirror under the falls, Conor gripping the other end, and the mirror began to shine brighter. A vibrant green light ignited.

Then Sky's legs bunched, and he launched himself into the air.

"Sky!" A scream caught in my throat as Sky vanished into the light… and into Clearwater's home.

Dad and Conor lowered the portal onto the bank, slowly, and an agonising few seconds passed before Sky jumped out. He landed at my side on all four paws and then rubbed against my leg as if he'd merely taken a nap instead of jumping through a portal to taunt a megalomaniacal fairy who wanted me dead.

"Sky," I hissed. "Was he there?"

"Miaow." Sky lifted his head then beckoned with a paw to follow him uphill, away from the lake.

"Blair, go with him," Dad told me. "We'll watch the portal. Clearwater is likely to be too suspicious to come through that way."

"I thought the whole intention was to lure him into a trap."

As Sky meowed impatiently, I resignedly followed him uphill. "Thanks for that, Sky."

"Miaow," he said, meaning, "you're welcome."

When I reached the top of the hill, I spied our enemy. Several winged figures appeared above the lake, while the witches on the shore lifted their wands in a challenge. Sky looked incredibly pleased with himself.

"I hope you know what you're doing, Sky." I scanned the winged figures, searching for my enemy, but Clearwater was nowhere in sight. *Is he hiding? Or—the portal.*

I turned to fly back downhill, but Sky reached out a paw and clawed me in the ankle. Biting back a curse, I looked more closely at the lake, and my gaze alighted on a figure who hovered apart from the others.

Clearwater.

My heart leapt into my throat. He was back in his fairy form, surveying our makeshift army with disdain. Holding the sceptre in one hand and the Seeing Stone in the other, he didn't give the lake a second's glance. He had no idea that my dad's home awaited on the other side.

How could he? He hadn't been here when my dad and I had gone into his sister's realm. But if I wasn't careful, he'd figure out my deception. I needed to get him to drop that Seeing Stone.

Our eyes locked across the water, and Clearwater's jaw tensed. "Blair Wilkes."

In response, I shot at him like a bullet, beating my wings as fast as they would move.

He lifted the sceptre, and a burst of light crashed into me before I hit my target. I heard someone shouting my name as my limbs flailed, pain rippling through my whole body. Not being able to control me with the Seeing Stone didn't mean he couldn't do serious damage, and it was all I could do to keep my wings beating, to keep myself from falling into the lake and ruining all chances we might have had of taking him by surprise.

Then a loud "MIAOW" shattered the air. I seized on the chance to catch my breath when Clearwater turned his head, distracted by the chorus of screeching fairy cats that had appeared on the lakeshore like some monstrous version of a choir.

"Get out of here," he spat, lifting the Seeing Stone.

The stone had no effect; if anything, the cats' screeching grew louder. I launched myself into flight again and managed to grab his arm, the one that held the sceptre. Clearwater's attention returned to me, and he effortlessly pulled his arm free of my grip. I wasn't strong enough to hold him.

I could manage a distraction, though. I snapped the fingers of my other hand, conjuring up a waterfall of glitter directly onto his head.

Clearwater merely narrowed his eyes in annoyance, but the fairy cats' shrieking reached a pitch that made my eardrums scream.

That was when my dad and Conor flew in behind, each seizing one of Clearwater's wings. He snarled in fury, waving the Seeing Stone, but the racket the fairy cats were making had already unbalanced him. I snapped my fingers and conjured up another illusion, this one of my cat. Clearwater barely twitched when the illusory Sky landed on his arm—but he'd failed to notice that the real Sky had glamoured himself into a giant.

With a roar, Sky leapt from the bank and collided with Clearwater's other arm. Before Clearwater could recover, the Seeing Stone flew out of his hand and plunged into the lake.

As the stone vanished below the surface, Clearwater shook his arm violently, dislodging Sky. My cat landed on his feet on the bank and sprang again. I threw myself at Clearwater, too.

This time he was unprepared. The three of us hit the

water, together with Conor and my dad, and we vanished below the surface.

Darkness closed in. I held my breath, grabbing for the nearest person, who turned out to be my cat. Sky dug his claws into my arm, making me yelp, and he yowled in annoyance himself when we surfaced in the lake on the other side.

My dad and Conor rose from the water, gripping Clearwater's beating wings, while Sky clung to me like a clawed and fluffy limpet. The pain from his sharp claws disoriented me so much that it took a moment for me to notice the army on the shore and the countless weapons pointed at us.

"What is this?" Clearwater yanked his wings free of my dad and Conor, his attention locking on a single figure at the head of the army. "Lady Eventide."

My dad's sister gave a wide smile at the sight of Clearwater's dawning realisation of his predicament. He still held the sceptre, but the Seeing Stone was out of reach, and he'd flown straight into an enemy's domain without his army.

"There's no running this time, Clearwater," she said. "I have wanted to see you brought to account for what you did to my family for a long time."

"The human world would like to have words with him too," my dad told her. "That said, we promised him to you, sister."

"My army will bring your castle to the ground," Clearwater snarled. "They'll follow me here."

"They can't get through the portal without an invitation from one of us." Dad flew behind him and seized the sceptre grip. Clearwater fought briefly, but the dozens of arrows pointing at him must have convinced him it wasn't worth putting up a struggle. "You've taken advantage of that loophole yourself often."

"Nobody is coming to help you, Clearwater," Lady Eventide told him. "I doubt your people were as keen to serve someone who hid among humans as they might have pretended."

"That, and he controlled them against their will," I added. "Luckily, the Seeing Stone is currently at the bottom of Fairy Falls's lake."

"How intriguing." Lady Eventide's eyes gleamed. "Pity it didn't come with you."

"We already made our bargain," Dad said firmly. "If you'll take Clearwater into custody, I'll bring the portal to you as promised."

"What about that?" She indicated the sceptre, which my dad held loosely in one hand.

"What?" Alarm filled my voice. "No!"

"Unfortunately, I seem to have already claimed this myself," said my dad. "Don't worry. I won't let it fall into the wrong hands."

Was he serious? I hadn't even thought about what might happen to the sceptre afterwards. I hadn't dared to think there might be an "afterwards" at all. Now, stunned relief took hold as I watched the fairies close in around Clearwater, herding him into the castle.

Lady Eventide lingered, eyeing my dad and Conor. "I shall expect that portal to be delivered shortly."

"Absolutely," Dad said. "I can trust you won't use it to declare war on Clearwater's remaining forces, can't I?"

"I'll give them a little time to recover from the shock of losing their leader again." A wide smile spread across her face, and she looked directly at me for the first time. "I believe that concludes our business, Blair. I thought you unworthy of being among us at first, but I stand corrected."

Blair. She'd called me Blair—and admitted to a mistake. This might just be a first in the entire history of the Eventide Court.

As if satisfied that she'd thoroughly stunned me, she gave

a last smile and followed her soldiers into the castle, where Clearwater awaited what I hoped would be a lifelong punishment.

We won.

My dad put an arm round me from behind. "It's over, Blair. Let's go home."

EPILOGUE

The goblin market was back in town. The sound of raucous laughter and music filled the background as I walked home from work to the witches' headquarters, the sky darkening overhead. Another reminder that summer was long over. The past four months had flown by, and I could hardly believe Samhain was already upon us.

The goblin market's cheerful music and the bright lights they'd parked on the lakeshore very much fit with the Halloween spirit, and I intended to go there later that evening, assuming the Head Witch ceremony didn't go south.

My nerves were already spiking, but I could only imagine how Rebecca felt. We both hoped she'd walk away from this without another year in service to the sceptre, but since we'd collectively decided that trying to repeat whatever Clearwater had done to that other sceptre was a bad idea, we'd had no choice but to abide by tradition and hope that the sceptre took the hint and chose someone else. Preferably someone *without* ambitions on the scale of Mrs Dailey's.

I entered the witches' headquarters and made my way to the council room. As I nudged the wooden door inward, heads turned to watch me enter. Self-conscious, I lowered my gaze as I found an empty seat. I knew most of the faces at the table by now, from the witches—including Aveline and her daughter—to the other paranormal heads like the were-wolves' pack chief and Vincent the vampire. Connor and my dad were there, too, representing the fairies. Not everyone was happy at them being invited to the meeting, but Madame Grey had made it clear that this wouldn't be a typical Head Witch ceremony, and they'd just have to deal with it.

"Good, our latecomer is here," said Aveline.

Thanks for that, Aveline. I'd stayed late at work as a favour to my boss, and I hadn't known everyone else would get here hours before the ceremony was due to start.

"Not just her." Veronica entered the room and shot me a smile as she took a seat beside me. "Shall we begin?"

A rush of gratitude towards my boss rose within me, not for the first time. It had been weird at first, going back to work after everything that had happened, but I'd been in dire need of some normality, and besides, the office was swamped. For one thing, there were an awful lot of hunters suddenly looking for new jobs, which was a minefield only Dritch & Co was equipped to handle.

"Yes, let's," said Madame Grey. "The current plan is for Rebecca to relinquish her sceptre and for it to choose its next wielder from a gathered audience."

"Of your own coven," added one of the visiting witches, a middle-aged redhead with a dress made of what appeared to be crow feathers. She seemed to have already dressed the part of Head Witch, though she wasn't the only person to come here with the assumption that she'd walk away with the sceptre.

"Your people were invited to town too," Madame Grey told her. "They refused."

"It was far too short notice," groused the witch.

Yeah, right. Madame Grey's face reflected my own scepticism as she replied. "It's Samhain, according to tradition. You've had plenty of time to prepare."

I'd expected this. While we'd put out an open invitation to any witch who wanted to sign up to be assessed by the sceptre, not many had come from outside of town. Evidently, the hopefuls who'd already been in the running hadn't wanted to invite witches from outside of their own covens to compete for a chance at the title of Head Witch. Madame Grey had conceded that it might be too much to hope for the other covens to be willing to depart from tradition, though my coworkers and I had tried to reach out to other covens who were usually excluded from the Head Witch ceremonies. But we'd already had our hands full, and it had been a little hard to put out a job advert for Head Witch without attracting crazies, as Veronica put it. In any case, this was an annual ceremony, so perhaps by next year, more people would be willing to listen.

Half the witches at the table had similar arguments to the first, which Madame Grey deflected with unending patience.

One, Aveline's daughter Vanessa, hesitantly asked the question everyone else had been thinking. "Whatever happened to the Seeing Stone?"

"It was lost in the fight," I told her and the other eagerly listening witches. "I believe Clearwater might have destroyed it."

Its actual location was unknown, but I'd seen a couple of merpeople children playing with what looked awfully like a crystal ball near the lake earlier that day. I wasn't *entirely* keen on the idea of leaving it open for being claimed by anyone who might happen upon it, but there was little chance that most people would recognise a Seeing Stone for what it was. I'd asked my dad to keep an eye out and prepare to figure out an alternative if someone realised the Seeing

Stone's location, but as of yet, we hadn't had anything to worry about on that front.

Mutters of discontent echoed up and down the table, but the witches accepted my explanation. It wasn't as if any of them had lie-sensing powers, after all.

"As to the matter of Head Witch…" Madame Grey rose to her feet. "I think it's best that we let the sceptre decide for itself, don't you?"

She swept out of the room, the other witches trailing in her wake. I waited for Rebecca, who looked nervous but determined as she joined the line of people leaving the room.

"Good luck," I whispered to her. "It'll be okay."

If the sceptre picked her again, we had a contingency plan that involved keeping her from participating in anything that might endanger her life or distract from her schoolwork, but I hoped we wouldn't need it. Rebecca had accomplished what the sceptre had chosen her to do, and in theory, it ought to be willing to pick someone else this time around.

There were certainly numerous options. The town hall was packed when we entered, and eyes followed us as we walked down the row of seats.

Seeing the panic in Rebecca's eyes, I reached out and squeezed her hand. "You've got this. The sceptre ought to know that you've fulfilled your mission."

She'd thwarted her mother and had opened the position to a lot more than just a handful of witches. I was proud of her. I hoped she knew that I always would be, Head Witch or not.

Alissa had saved me a seat, and I joined her. We watched Rebecca walk the short distance to the front of the room, where Madame Grey waited to begin the ceremony. Blythe sat on my other side and gave me a grunt of acknowledgement, her gaze fixed on her sister.

As silence fell, Madame Grey called the ceremony to

start. Despite my efforts to calm myself, my nerves began buzzing again. There were plenty of other witches present, but what if the sceptre picked Rebecca after all? Or worse? Aveline was here, as was her daughter, and other witches who'd purposefully excluded other covens from their regions from being invited.

I hardly heard any of Madame Grey's speech and only tuned in when Rebecca herself took the stage. I was proud of her for not shaking—at least not visibly—when she held the sceptre aloft.

"The sceptre will now choose the next wielder," she announced.

Purple light spilled out, and I held my breath as the sceptre's light fell on the audience. The light played across the crowd, narrowing to a single spot… me.

My heart sank. *Please, not me.* I didn't need the responsibility, and honestly, I just wanted some peace for once. But if it wasn't Rebecca, I'd have to—wait.

The light wasn't pointing at me, but it shined over my shoulder, alighting on… *Blythe.*

Rebecca's eyes widened as she saw it too, but her sister didn't move. She was in shock, I assumed.

"Go on." I nudged Blythe. "Go to your sister."

She rose to her feet while the crowd erupted in chatter and speculation. I didn't hear what Rebecca said to her sister when she handed over the sceptre, but I had to admit to feeling a rush of relief mingling with my own shock and confusion.

"Blythe?" Alissa whispered. "Seriously?"

"Better than Aveline." *I think.* Blythe was notoriously self-centred, but she'd need to learn some self-control if she was going to spend the next year mired in tedious meetings. Who knew? Maybe it would be good for her.

Blythe, though. Seriously?

As the ceremony drew to a close, I left the hall with the chattering crowd. Everyone seemed to be discussing the new development. I gathered that Blythe wasn't particularly popular, but I almost felt sorry for her after hearing some of the comments.

"I can't believe it was her," said Bethan. "You don't think she'll do a good job, do you, Blair?"

"You know, I think she will." I raised my voice, unable to believe I was defending her. "She's sat in on Rebecca's lessons for months, she's pretty much out of a job already, and she's used to people not liking her."

Too late, I realised Blythe herself was behind us. *Oops.* I held my breath when her eyes met mine, a scowl on her lips.

"Just as long as it's not my sister," the new Head Witch said.

As she walked away, I covered my face with a groan. "I didn't mean for her to hear that."

"Blair." Rebecca came up and hugged me, burying her head in my shoulder. "Everyone's still staring at me."

"Because you're a former Head Witch, and you did a better job than certain other people I could mention." I didn't bother lowering my voice when I saw Aveline nearby. "I told you things would be fine, didn't I?"

She could go back to school, and her mother would never interfere in her life again. Last I'd heard, Mrs Dailey had been transferred back to the LPFP under new management, and Madame Grey herself had seen to it that the witches had assumed temporary leadership of the hunters until they sorted themselves out. Really, I had to laugh at the irony.

Behind Aveline, I spied Madame Grey approaching.

Rebecca let go of me when she saw her too. "Madame Grey, thank you. For everything."

"It was my pleasure," Madame Grey said, her tone almost fond. "Blair, I'm glad to see you."

"What do you think of Blythe as a candidate?" I asked curiously. "I mean, she'd be better than me…"

"Better than you?" she echoed. "I must disagree, but I think you've had quite enough excitement already, don't you?"

"Yeah, I guess." I smiled. "We'll have to see how it turns out." At least everyone had been given a fair shot this time.

While the chattering crowd dispersed, I found Nathan waiting for me, and he greeted me with a kiss. "Ready for our date?"

"Definitely." The Troll's Tavern was only a short distance away, and there was a fair chance it'd be packed with witches who'd attended the ceremony, but it was our first date as just the two of us in a while. As much as I liked spending time around Erin and Buck—and my foster parents when they visited—I'd been craving time alone with him.

Nathan and I chatted over our meals, speculating on the future of the Head Witch title now that Blythe was the sceptre's wielder and not Rebecca.

"I feel kind of bad for her," I whispered to him across the table. "She hates attention. But considering all the other ways this might have gone wrong…"

He tilted his head. "You thought you might end up being chosen yourself, didn't you?"

"I hoped not," I admitted. "I don't need any more crap. I can imagine the Head Witch council having a collective screaming fit if they found out a half fairy got chosen to wield one of their sceptres."

"If you ask me, they'd deserve it," he commented. "I don't blame you for wanting to sit this one out, though. Your dad already has a sceptre, right?"

"Yes, but he doesn't use it." Only Madame Grey knew where it was, and she'd led the rest of the council to believe the sceptre had been lost along with the Seeing Stone. Probably for the best, given that nobody knew how to undo what Clearwater had done to enable the sceptre to be used by anyone who picked it up.

"I know," said Nathan. "Believe me. My father asked where it was, and I'm not sure he bought my excuse for not knowing."

"Why would he want to know?" The Harker family and I weren't exactly at odds, not anymore. In fact, his family and my foster parents had actually met in person a few weeks ago. I'd expected no end of awkwardness, but weirdly enough, Nathan's family had spent long enough in the normal world that my foster parents were positively acceptable compared to my fairy and witch heritage. They'd talked about camping, of all things.

"Curiosity, I assume," he replied. "He's keeping an eye on the situation here. He's mentioned coming out of retirement too."

I raised a brow. "Not to work for the hunters?"

"He's better than some of the other possible options."

"True." Hunters had quit in droves, but plenty remained. Some of them held out hope for the return of their leader, but the last we'd seen of Clearwater, he'd been surrounded by armed fairies in the Court of Eventide. I had an inkling that the fairies' idea of a prison might well put the LPFP to shame, and he deserved no less.

Hours later, Nathan and I left the pub hand in hand, backed by the strident howls of the werewolf band playing at the New Moon.

"I think they might have actually improved since I last heard them," I remarked. When Nathan made a sceptical noise, I added, "Nah, I take it back. They're still terrible."

He laughed under his breath and squeezed my hand. "Ready to go home?"

"I have to see my dad first," I reminded him. "We won't be long. It's the last night of the market."

"Of course," he said with a smile. "I'll see you later."

I kissed him goodbye and began to make my way towards the lake. I'd waited for this night for months, and my pulse fluttered with anticipation when I saw my dad waiting for me near the water. The dark surface of the lake reflected the violet glow of the sceptre he held in one hand.

"Ready?" he asked.

I inclined my head. "Yeah."

The lights of the goblin market beckoned, but we'd go there later. We had one more stop to make first.

My dad led the way through the forest, but not to the fairies' part of the woods, though the path had been returned to its former spot after we'd defeated Clearwater. Soon, we reached the clearing wherein lay the cottage he'd once shared with my mother.

A lump grew in my throat when we approached the gate, which my dad opened with his free hand. In the other, the sceptre glowed faintly purple, illuminating the overgrown garden. It was strange seeing the instrument in my dad's hand; until now, he'd never used the sceptre, and with luck, he wouldn't have to do so again. This was a one-off.

"Is this all I have to do?" He held out the sceptre, letting its light shine over the cottage and the worn bricks that might have been my home, in another life.

I took in a shaky breath. "Yeah. The sceptre will do the rest."

Light split the air, and a ghostly figure appeared, shimmering, above the ground. My mother, looking as solid as if she was alive.

"Braden?" Disbelief shrouded her voice when she saw my dad and me. "You... how can you be here?"

"Blair," he said simply.

My mother smiled at me, tears shining in her eyes. "You're remarkable."

Eyes stinging, I smiled back, the lump in my throat preventing me from speaking. Dad stepped towards her, his hand outstretched, and I moved back to give them some privacy.

My mother shook her head. "Blair, come here."

I stepped up, letting her wrap her arms around me and my dad. Tears flowed freely from my eyes.

All too soon, she let go. "I can't stay. You know that, don't you?" she said tenderly.

"Of course." Dad drew in a ragged breath. "It's… it's good to see you, Tanith."

I swallowed and nodded. The sceptre might have been a world of trouble, but I'd never forget the gift it'd given us: a chance to be a family again, if just for a short time. "I'm glad. I wish…"

"Don't." Mum extended her finger to my lips, and I shivered at her ghostly touch. "Don't wish for things to be different, Blair. It won't do you any good. This is your life, and you deserve to live every minute to the full."

I crumpled, tears streaming down my face, even though I knew she was right. "I know. One night out of the year is better than none."

"It's a gift nobody can take from us," Dad said. "I'll never forget that."

"Nor me." I leaned on him, drinking in every moment of my mother's presence, until she faded into the night.

When we left the garden, Sky waited for me at the gate, and he brushed against my ankles as I walked, my heart full and aching at once.

"Miaow," he said.

I crouched to give him a stroke. "Miaow yourself." I

straightened upright and smiled at my dad. "Want to go and see the markets?"

"Of course."

We carried onward, Sky padding in front of us, as we walked towards the sound of laughter and the rush of the waterfall.

ABOUT THE AUTHOR

Elle Adams lives in the middle of England, where she spends most of her time reading an ever-growing mountain of books, planning her next adventure, or writing. Elle's books are humorous mysteries with a paranormal twist, packed with magical mayhem.

She also writes urban and contemporary fantasy novels as Emma L. Adams.

Visit http://www.elleadamsauthor.com/ to find out more about Elle's books.